USBORNE KEY SKILLS

Practice Pad
Subtracting

Written by Sam Smith

Illustrated by Maddie Frost

Designed by Laura Hammonds,
Winsome d'Abreu and
Carly Davies

Series Editor: Felicity Brooks

Shhh!

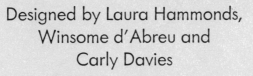

10 − 3 = 7

Once you've completed an activity sheet from this pad,
you can check it using the answer pages at the back.

Here are the animals you'll meet in this pad.

You can tear off the sheets to take out with you for practice wherever you are.

Coco the raccoon

Bun the rabbit

Olly the owl

Foxy the fox

Mo the mouse

Moley the mole

Squilly the squirrel

Hug the bear

Stripe the badger

Spike the hedgehog

Note to grown-ups: the term 'less' relates to amounts that are measured rather than counted, e.g. an amount of a liquid. The correct term for countable objects is 'fewer', but this term is not as commonly used with children, so 'less' is used throughout this pad.

Number order

Starting at 10, join up the numbers in order, from highest to lowest, to finish drawing the string of Bun's kite.

Number names

Hug is matching each number to its name.
Finish drawing the lines for him.

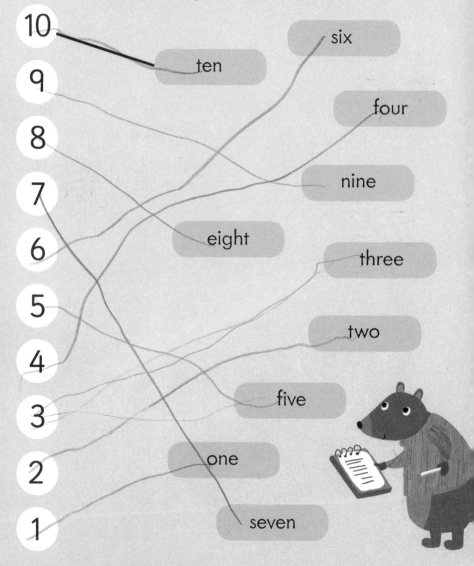

Subtract 1

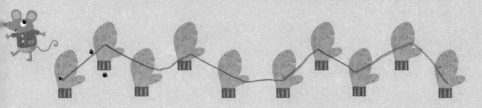

3

Count the mittens in each group below, then cross out 1 of them. Write the numbers in the boxes.

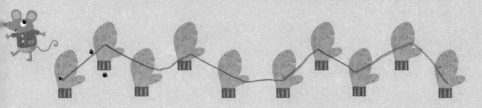

How many mittens above?   Subtract   1 of the mittens.   How many mittens left?

10   –   1   9   0

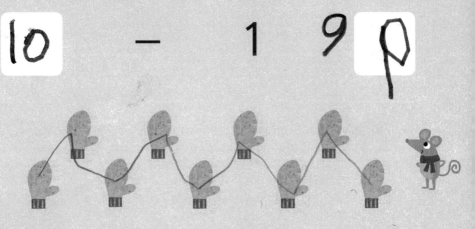

How many mittens above?   Subtract   1 of the mittens.   How many mittens left?

9   –   1   8

Subtract 1

Count the leaves in each group below, then cross out 1 of them. Write the numbers in the boxes.

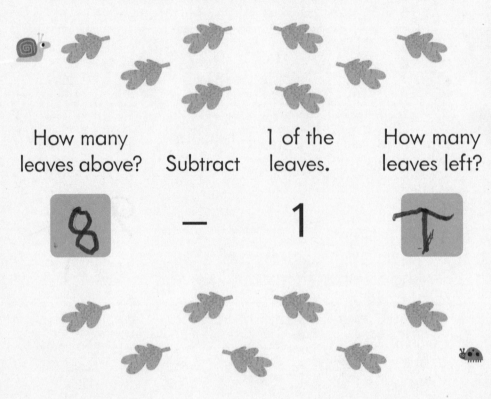

How many leaves above?	Subtract	1 of the leaves.	How many leaves left?
8	–	1	7

How many leaves above?	Subtract	1 of the leaves.	How many leaves left?
7	–	1	6

Subtract 1

Count the bees in each group below, then cross out 1 of them. Write the numbers in the boxes.

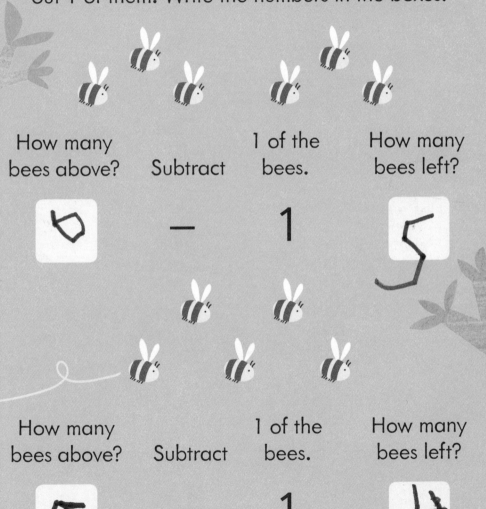

How many bees above? | Subtract | 1 of the bees. | How many bees left?

6 − 1 5

How many bees above? | Subtract | 1 of the bees. | How many bees left?

5 − 1 4

Subtract 1

Count the apples in each group below, then cross
out 1 of them. Write the numbers in the boxes.

How many
apples above? Subtract 1 of the apples. How many apples left?

  — 1 3

How many
apples above? Subtract 1 of the apples. How many apples left?

  — 1

Subtract 1

Count the cakes in each group below, then cross out 1 of them. Write the numbers in the boxes.

| How many cakes above? | Subtract | 1 of the cakes. | How many cakes left? |

2   –   1   1

| How many cakes above? | Subtract | 1 of the cakes. | How many cakes left? |

1   –   1   0

Subtract 2

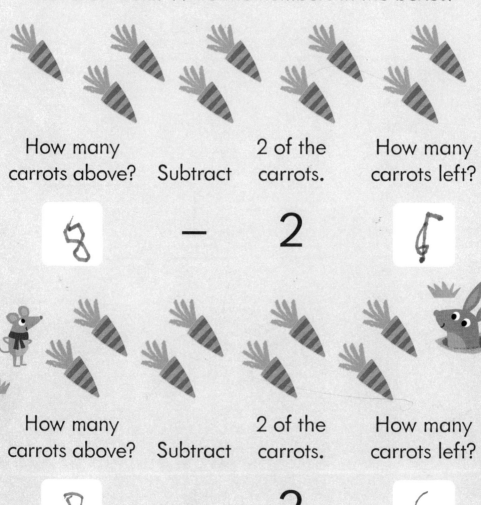

Count the carrots in each group below, then cross out 2 of them. Write the numbers in the boxes.

How many carrots above? Subtract 2 of the carrots. How many carrots left?

8 − 2 6

How many carrots above? Subtract 2 of the carrots. How many carrots left?

8 − 2 6

Subtract 2

Count the berries in each group below, then cross out 2 of them. Write the numbers in the boxes.

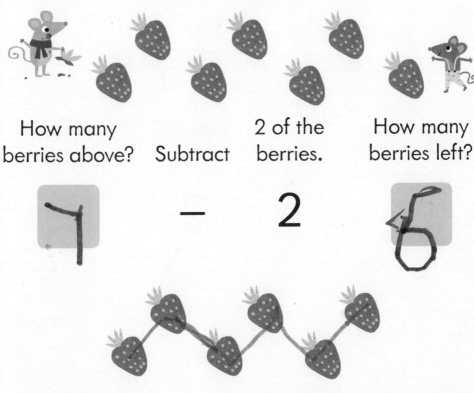

How many berries above?

Subtract

2 of the berries.

How many berries left?

7   −   2   6

How many berries above?

Subtract

2 of the berries.

How many berries left?

6   −   2   4

Subtract 2

Count the rings in each group below, then cross out 2 of them. Write the numbers in the boxes.

How many rings above?	Subtract	2 of the rings.	How many rings left?

5   −   2   

How many rings above?	Subtract	2 of the rings.	How many rings left?

     −   2

Subtract 2

Count the cups in each group below, then cross out 2 of them. Write the numbers in the boxes.

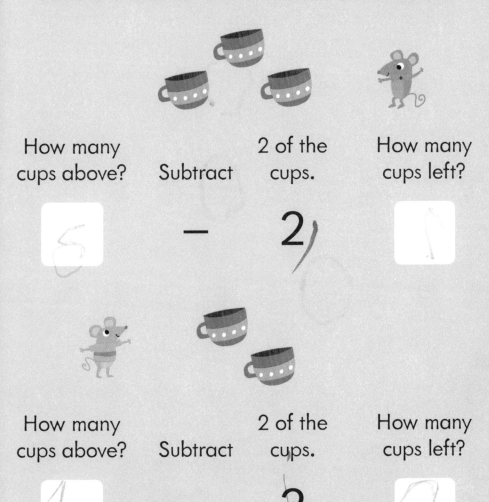

How many cups above?

Subtract

2 of the cups.

How many cups left?

6 − 2)

How many cups above?

Subtract

2 of the cups.

How many cups left?

1 − 2

Number lines

Help Coco to subtract 1 from each number in red.
Start at the number in red on each number line, then
count back one. Circle the number you reach.

1 · 2 · 3 · 4 · 5 · (6) · 7 · 8 · 9 · 10

1 · 2 · 3 · 4 · 5 · (6) · 7 · 8 · 9 · 10

1 · 2 · 3 · (4) · 5 · 6 · 7 · 8 · 9 · 10

1 · 2 · 3 · 4 · 5 · 6 · 7 · 8 · 9 · (10)

Thanks for your help!

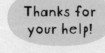

Number lines

13

Help Moley to count back 2 from each
number in red, and circle the
number you reach.

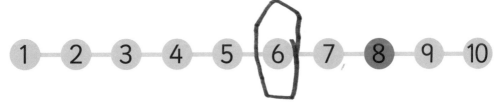

1 — 2 — 3 — 4 — 5 — 6 — 7 — 8 — 9 — 10

1 — 2 — 3 — 4 — 5 — 6 — 7 — 8 — 9 — 10

1 — 2 — 3 — 4 — 5 — 6 — 7 — 8 — 9 — 10

1 — 2 — 3 — 4 — 5 — 6 — 7 — 8 — 9 — 10

-2

More subtracting

Count the shells in each group below, then cross out
how many to subtract. Write the numbers in the boxes.

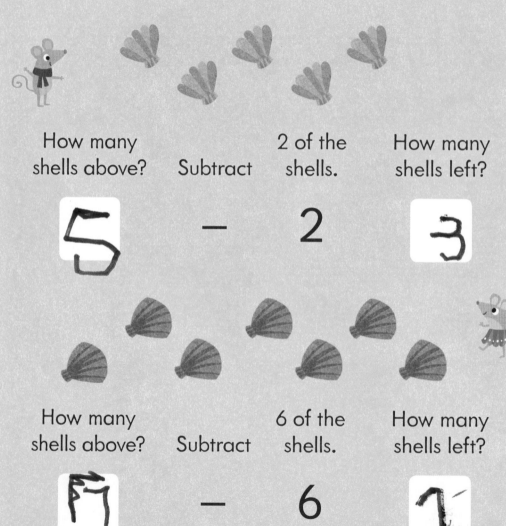

How many
shells above?   Subtract   2 of the
                              shells.   How many
                                           shells left?

5   –   2   3

How many
shells above?   Subtract   6 of the
                              shells.   How many
                                           shells left?

7   –   6   1

More subtracting

Cross out how many books to subtract from each group and write the numbers in the boxes.

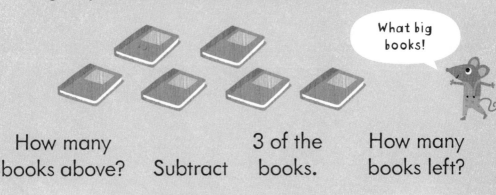

What big books!

How many books above?	Subtract	3 of the books.	How many books left?

– 3

How many books above?	Subtract	8 of the books.	How many books left?

– 8

More subtracting

Count the socks in each group below, then cross out
how many to subtract. Write the numbers in the boxes.

These aren't
my socks...

How many socks above?	Subtract	5 of the socks.	How many socks left?

$\boxed{}$ $-$ 5 $\boxed{}$

How many socks above?	Subtract	1 of the socks.	How many socks left?

$\boxed{1}$ $-$ 1 $\boxed{1}$

More subtracting

Cross out how many gifts to subtract from each group and write the numbers in the boxes.

 I wonder what's inside!

How many gifts above?	Subtract	9 of the gifts.	How many gifts left?

 — 9 =

How many gifts above?	Subtract	4 of the gifts.	How many gifts left?

 — 4

More subtracting

Count the fish in each group below, then cross out
how many to subtract. Write the numbers in the boxes.

How many fish above?	Subtract	10 of the fish.	How many fish left?

1   −   10

How many fish above?	Subtract	7 of the fish.	How many fish left?

    −   7

Number lines

Help Bun to subtract 3 from each number in red.
Start at the number in red on each number line, then
count back three. Circle the number you reach.

1 — 2 — 3 — 4 — 5 — **6** — 7 — 8 — 9 — 10

1 — 2 — 3 — 4 — 5 — 6 — 7 — **8** — 9 — 10

1 — 2 — 3 — 4 — 5 — 6 — 7 — 8 — 9 — **10**

1 — 2 — 3 — 4 — **5** — 6 — 7 — 8 — 9 — 10

-3

You're good
at this!

Number lines

Help Foxy to count back 4 from each
number in red, and circle the
number you reach.

1 — 2 — 3 — 4 — 5 — 6 — 7 — 8 — 9 — 10

1 — 2 — 3 — 4 — 5 — 6 — 7 — 8 — 9 — 10

1 — 2 — 3 — 4 — 5 — 6 — 7 — 8 — 9 — 10

1 — 2 — 3 — 4 — 5 — 6 — 7 — 8 — 9 — 10

Who has less?

21

Each animal has a different number of apples in their basket. Draw a circle around any animal who has less than Squilly.

Squilly

Odd or even?

Write the answer to each calculation in the empty box and circle 'odd' or 'even' below each number. Use the number line at the bottom to help you.

5 – **1** = 6

odd / even   odd / even   odd / even

2 – **1** =

odd / even   odd / even   odd / even

7 – **1** =

odd / even   odd / even   odd / even

1 – 2 – 3 – 4 – 5 – 6 – 7 – 8 – 9 – 10

odd   even   odd   even   odd   even   odd   even   odd   even

Odd or even?

Write the answer to each calculation in the empty box and circle 'odd' or 'even' below each number. Use the number line at the bottom to help you.

6 – **2** = *8*

odd / even   odd / even   odd / even

9 – **2** = *7*

odd / even   odd / even   odd / even

3 – **2** = *1*

odd / even   odd / even   odd / even

1 – 2 – 3 – 4 – 5 – 6 – 7 – 8 – 9 – 10

odd even odd even odd even odd even odd even

Write 1 less

What is 1 less than each of these numbers?
Write the answers in the boxes next to them.

2	2		10	10
7	7		5	5
9	9		8	8
3	3		1	7
6	6		4	4

Write 2 less

What is 2 less than each of these numbers?
Write the answers in the boxes next to them.

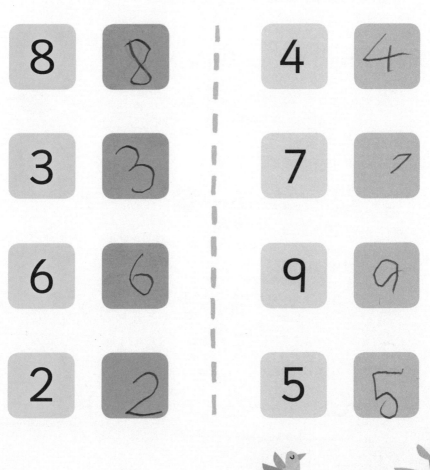

8	8		4	4
3	3		7	7
6	6		9	9
2	2		5	5

For each number line, read how many Stripe needs to subtract from the number in red, then count back and circle the number you reach.

Subtract 7 from the number in red.

1 — 2 — 3 — 4 — 5 — 6 — 7 — 8 — ⑨ — 10

Subtract 3 this time.

1 — 2 — 3 — 4 — 5 — ⑥ — 7 — 8 — 9 — 10

Subtract 5 this time.

1 — 2 — 3 — 4 — 5 — 6 — 7 — 8 — 9 — ⑩

Subtract 1 this time.

1 — 2 — ③ — 4 — 5 — 6 — 7 — 8 — 9 — 10

Hello there, little bird!

Number lines

For each number line, help Squilly to count
back from the number in red, and
circle the number you reach.

Subtract 4 from the number in red.

1 — 2 — 3 — 4 — (5) — 6 — 7 — 8 — 9 — 10

Subtract 7 this time.

1 — 2 — 3 — 4 — 5 — 6 — 7 — 8 — 9 — (10)

Subtract 2 this time.

1 — 2 — 3 — (4) — 5 — 6 — 7 — 8 — 9 — 10

Subtract 3 this time.

1 — 2 — 3 — 4 — 5 — 6 — (7) — 8 — 9 — 10

Number lines

For each number line, read how many Bun needs to subtract from the number in red, then count back and circle the number you reach.

Subtract 2 from the number in red.

Subtract 4 this time.

Subtract 1 this time.

Subtract 5 this time.

Hmm, let's see...

Number lines

For each number line, help Foxy and his friend
to count back from the number in red,
and circle the number you reach.

Subtract 5 from the number in red.

1 — 2 — 3 — 4 — 5 — 6 — 7 — 8 — (9) — 10

Subtract 2 this time.

1 — 2 — (3) — 4 — 5 — 6 — 7 — 8 — 9 — 10

Subtract 4 this time.

1 — 2 — 3 — 4 — 5 — 6 — (7) — 8 — 9 — 10

Subtract 6 this time.

1 — 2 — 3 — 4 — 5 — 6 — 7 — (8) — 9 — 10

The right order

Mark these calculations to see if the numbers in them are in the right order. Put a ✔ or a **X** in each box. Try crossing out the fruit to help you.

5 – 3 = 2

3 – 5 = 2 ☐

7 – 4 = 3

4 – 7 = 3 ☐

8 – 2 = 6

2 – 8 = 6 ☐

The right order

Mark these calculations to see if the numbers in them
are in the right order. Put a ✔ or a **X** in each box.
Try crossing out the fruit to help you.

9 – 7 = 2 ☐

7 – 9 = 2 ☐

2 – 6 = 4 ☐

6 – 2 = 4 ☐

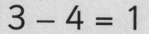

3 – 4 = 1 ☐

4 – 3 = 1 ☐

The right order

32

Mark these calculations to see if the numbers in them
are in the right order. Put a ✔ or a **X** in each box.
Try crossing out the fruit to help you.

10 – 7 = 3 ▢

7 – 10 = 3 ▢

9 – 4 = 5 ▢

4 – 9 = 5 ▢

4 – 2 = 2 ▢

2 – 4 = 2 ▢

The right order

Mark these calculations to see if the numbers in them
are in the right order. Put a ✔ or a **X** in each box.
Try crossing out the fruit to help you.

$3 - 9 = 6$ ☐

$9 - 3 = 6$ ☐

$5 - 2 = 3$ ☐

$2 - 5 = 3$ ☐

$10 - 1 = 9$ ☐

$1 - 10 = 9$ ☐

Balance beams

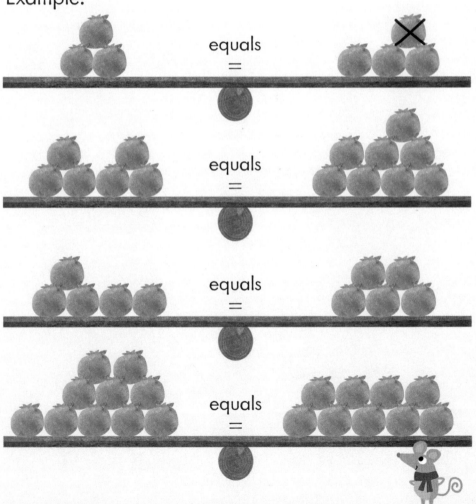

To balance, these beams should have the same number of oranges on each side. Count the oranges – if one side has more, cross out oranges from that side.

Example:

equals
=

equals
=

equals
=

equals
=

Balance beams

Count the cupcakes on each beam.
If one side has more, cross out
cupcakes from that side.

Example:

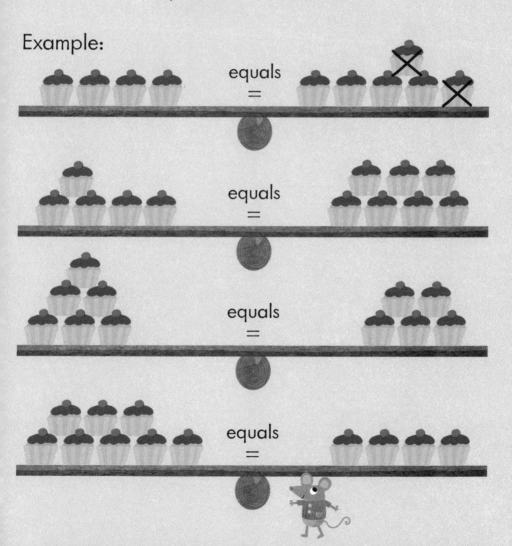

Balance beams

36

To balance, these beams should have the same number of acorns on each side. Count the acorns – if one side has more, cross out acorns from that side.

Example:

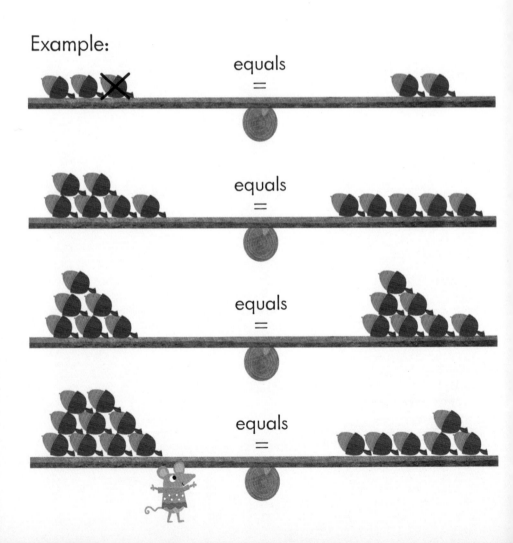

Balance beams

Count the teacups on each beam.
If one side has more, cross out
teacups from that side.

Example:

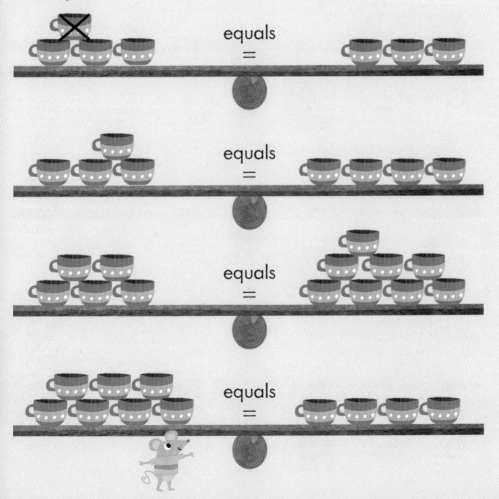

Balance beams

For each beam, cross out the number of marbles shown i
red below it. Then draw marbles on the other side of the
beam until it balances, and complete the calculation.

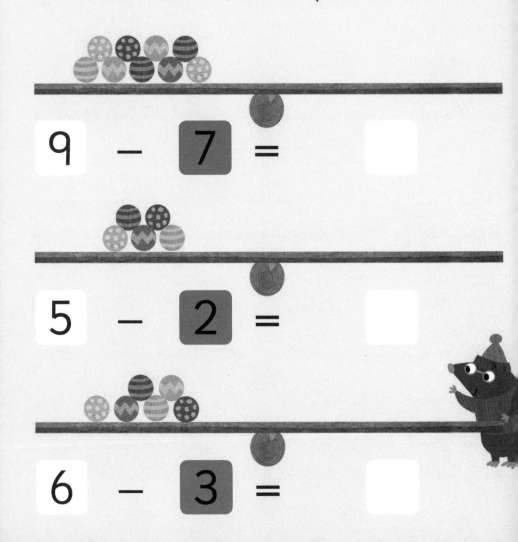

$9 - 7 =$ [ ]

$5 - 2 =$ [ ]

$6 - 3 =$ [ ]

Balance beams

For each beam, cross out the number of mushrooms shown in red below it. Then draw mushrooms on the other side of the beam until it balances, and complete the calculation.

7 – 6 =

8 – 3 =

4 – 1 =

Balance beams

For each beam, cross out the number of gifts shown in red below it. Then draw gifts on the other side of the beam until it balances, and complete the calculation.

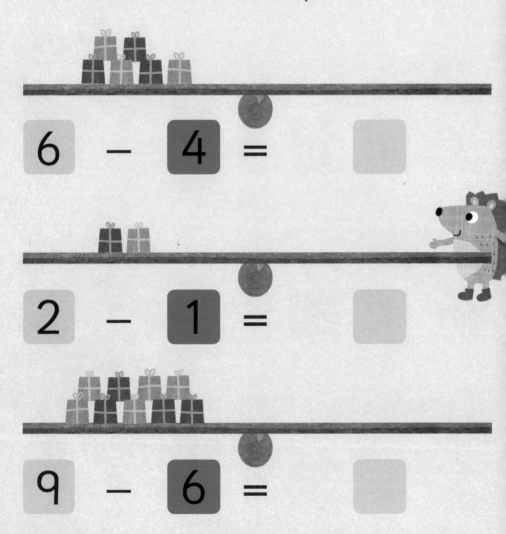

$6 - 4 =$

$2 - 1 =$

$9 - 6 =$

Balance beams

For each beam, cross out the number of watermelon slices shown in red below it. Then draw slices on the other side of the beam until it balances, and complete the calculation.

$5 - 3 =$

$7 - 4 =$

$3 - 2 =$

Number lines

Help Moley to count back from the number in red on each number line to find the answers to the calculations. Write the answers on the dotted lines.

$4 - 2 =$ ....

0 — 1 — 2 — 3 — **4** — 5 — 6 — 7 — 8 — 9

$6 - 5 =$ ....

0 — 1 — 2 — 3 — 4 — 5 — **6** — 7 — 8 — 9

$7 - 4 =$ ....

0 — 1 — 2 — 3 — 4 — 5 — 6 — **7** — 8 — 9

$3 - 3 =$ ....

0 — 1 — 2 — **3** — 4 — 5 — 6 — 7 — 8 — 9

Number lines

Help Spike to count back from each number in red, and write the answers to the calculations on the dotted lines.

3 − 2 = ...

0 — 1 — 2 — **3** — 4 — 5 — 6 — 7 — 8 — 9

8 − 5 = ...

0 — 1 — 2 — 3 — 4 — 5 — 6 — 7 — **8** — 9

6 − 4 = ...

0 — 1 — 2 — 3 — 4 — 5 — **6** — 7 — 8 — 9

2 − 1 = ...

0 — 1 — **2** — 3 — 4 — 5 — 6 — 7 — 8 — 9

Yummy!

Number lines

Help Foxy to count back from the number in red
on each number line to find the answers to the
calculations. Write the answers on the dotted lines.

$1 - 1 = $.......

0 — **1** — 2 — 3 — 4 — 5 — 6 — 7 — 8 — 9

$5 - 4 = $.......

0 — 1 — 2 — 3 — 4 — **5** — 6 — 7 — 8 — 9

$9 - 5 = $.......

0 — 1 — 2 — 3 — 4 — 5 — 6 — 7 — 8 — **9**

$7 - 2 = $.......

0 — 1 — 2 — 3 — 4 — 5 — 6 — **7** — 8 — 9

Number lines

Help Coco to count back from each number
in red, and write the answers to the
calculations on the dotted lines.

$4 - 4 =$ ....

0 – 1 – 2 – 3 – **4** – 5 – 6 – 7 – 8 – 9

$8 - 6 =$ ....

0 – 1 – 2 – 3 – 4 – 5 – 6 – 7 – **8** – 9

$7 - 3 =$ ....

0 – 1 – 2 – 3 – 4 – 5 – 6 – **7** – 8 – 9

$5 - 2 =$ ....

0 – 1 – 2 – 3 – 4 – **5** – 6 – 7 – 8 – 9

That's a tricky one!

Picture subtracting

Fill in how many gifts are on each table. Cross out the number of gifts to subtract, then write how many are left

$\square$ − 5 = $\square$

gifts on table gifts gifts left

$\square$ − 3 = $\square$

gifts on table gifts gifts left

$\square$ − 6 = $\square$

gifts on table gifts gifts left

Picture subtracting

Fill in how many cupcakes are on each table. Cross out the
umber of cupcakes to subtract, then write how many are left.

☐ – **4** = ☐

cupcakes on table   cupcakes   cupcakes left

☐ – **1** = ☐

cupcakes on table   cupcakes   cupcakes left

☐ – **7** = ☐

cupcakes on table   cupcakes   cupcakes left

Picture subtracting

Count the fruit on each shelf, then cross out the number
of them the mice want to buy. Fill in the numbers, and
write how many are left to complete the calculations.

Picture subtracting

Count the fruit on each shelf, then cross out the number
of them the mice want to buy. Fill in the numbers, and
write how many are left to complete the calculations.

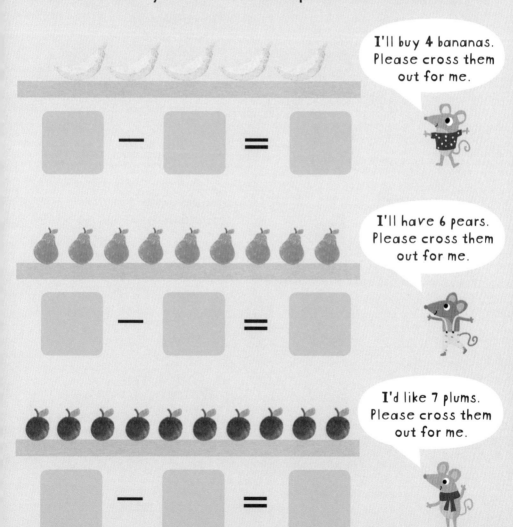

Picture subtracting

Fill in how many butterflies Mo can see. Then write how many have flown away, and how many butterflies are lef

Picture subtracting

Fill in how many bees Mo can see. Then write how many have flown away, and how many bees are left.

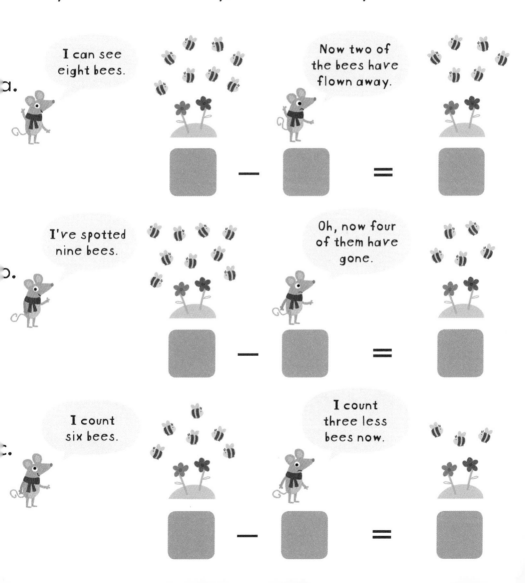

Number lines

For each number line, count back from the number in red to help you complete the calculation. Then circle whether the answer is 'odd' or 'even'.

$3 - 1 =$ ....   odd / even

1 — 2 — **3** — 4 — 5 — 6 — 7 — 8 — 9 — 10

$7 - 4 =$ ....   odd / even

1 — 2 — 3 — 4 — 5 — 6 — **7** — 8 — 9 — 10

$10 - 5 =$ ....   odd / even

1 — 2 — 3 — 4 — 5 — 6 — 7 — 8 — 9 — **10**

$6 - 2 =$ ....   odd / even

1 — 2 — 3 — 4 — 5 — **6** — 7 — 8 — 9 — 10

Number lines

For each number line, count back from the number in red to help you complete the calculation. Then circle whether the answer is 'odd' or 'even'.

$9 - 6 =$ ....   odd / even

1 — 2 — 3 — 4 — 5 — 6 — 7 — 8 — 9 — 10

$4 - 3 =$ ....   odd / even

1 — 2 — 3 — 4 — 5 — 6 — 7 — 8 — 9 — 10

$5 - 2 =$ ....   odd / even

1 — 2 — 3 — 4 — 5 — 6 — 7 — 8 — 9 — 10

$8 - 4 =$ ....   odd / even

1 — 2 — 3 — 4 — 5 — 6 — 7 — 8 — 9 — 10

Subtracting quiz

Help Foxy to fill in the answers to
these calculations in the boxes.

7 − 3 =

5 − 4 =

9 − 5 =

6 − 3 =

8 − 6 =

4 − 1 =

Subtracting quiz

Now help Coco to fill in the
answers to these calculations.

7 − 1 =

6 − 5 =

8 − 4 =

7 − 5 =

Right, then...

5 − 3 =

9 − 6 =

Subtracting nothing

Help Stripe and Spike to fill in the answers
to these calculations in the boxes.

$6 - 0 =$

$3 - 0 =$

$9 - 0 =$

$7 - 0 =$

$1 - 0 =$

Subtracting everything

Now help Moley to fill in the answers
to these calculations.

8 – 8 =

4 – 4 =

2 – 2 =

7 – 7 =

5 – 5 =

Find the difference

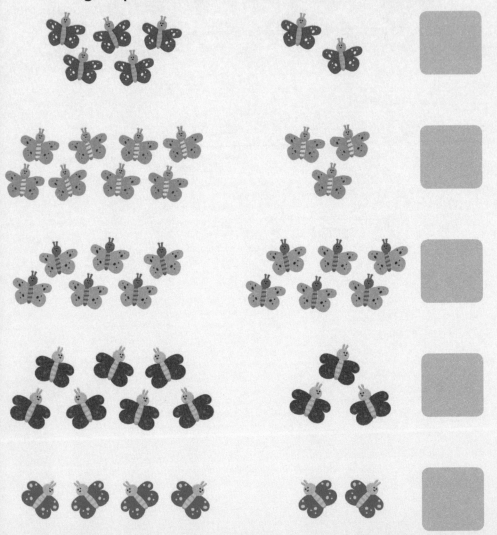

58

For each type of butterfly, find the difference between the number of butterflies in the two groups. Write the answers in the boxes.

Find the difference

For each type of book, find the difference
between the number of books in the two
groups. Write the answers in the boxes.

Find the difference

For each type of flower, find the difference
between the number of flowers in the two
groups. Write the answers in the boxes.

Find the difference

61

For each type of T-shirt, find the difference between the number of T-shirts in the two groups. Write the answers in the boxes.

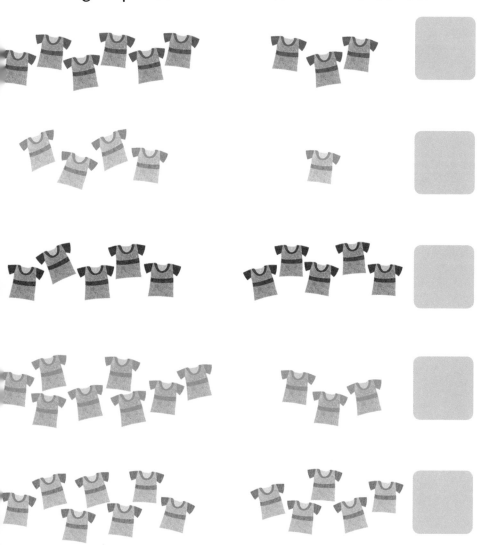

Difference game

The numbers that each pair of animals is holding must have a difference of 3. For each pair, write the lower number that's missing.

6

10

4

3

7

9

1 2 3 4 5 6 7 8 9 10

Find the difference

Each hoop scores one point. Find the difference between each pair's scores. Use the number line at the bottom to count back from the higher score to the lower score.

Moley's score

Spike's score

difference

Coco's score

Foxy's score

difference

1 — 2 — 3 — 4 — 5 — 6 — 7 — 8 — 9 — 10

Find the difference

The animals are playing hoops again. Find the difference between each pair's scores, using the number line to help you.

Moley's score

Spike's score

difference

Coco's score

Foxy's score

difference

1 — 2 — 3 — 4 — 5 — 6 — 7 — 8 — 9 — 10

Find the difference

Find the difference between Squilly and Hug's scores for each pair of targets. Use the number line at the bottom to count back from the higher score to the lower score.

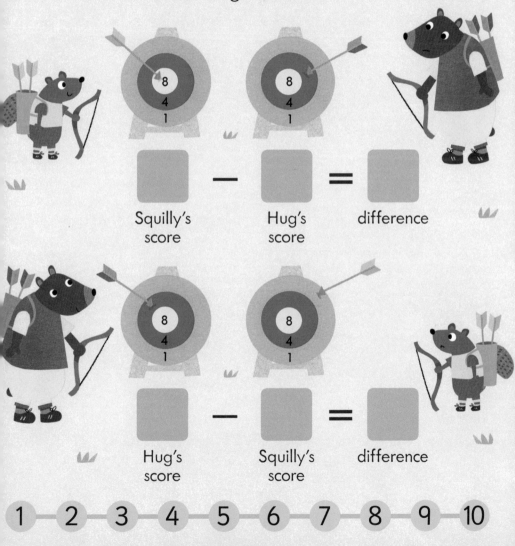

Squilly's score — Hug's score = difference

Hug's score — Squilly's score = difference

1 2 3 4 5 6 7 8 9 10

Find the difference

Squilly and Hug are taking another turn. Find the difference between their scores for each pair of targets, using the number line to help you.

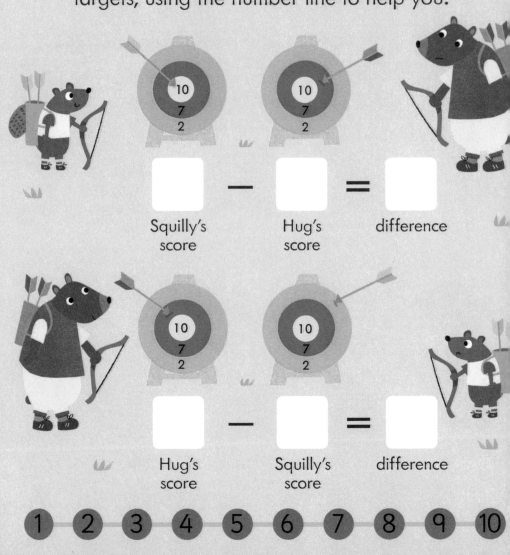

Squilly's score — Hug's score = difference

Hug's score — Squilly's score = difference

Same difference

Write the animals' long jump scores in the correct boxes in each calculation. Then count along the number line to find the difference, and write it in the green boxes.

Count **back** from Foxy's score to Coco's score...

☐ — ☐ = ☐

Foxy's score   Coco's score   difference

Count **forward** from Coco's score to Foxy's score...

☐ + ☐ = ☐

Coco's score   difference   Foxy's score

1 — 2 — 3 — 4 — 5 — 6 — 7 — 8 — 9 — 10

Same difference

The animals are jumping again. Write their scores in the correct boxes in each calculation. Then count along the number line to write the difference in the blue boxes.

Count **back** from Foxy's score to Coco's score...

$$\boxed{} - \boxed{} = \boxed{}$$

Foxy's score   Coco's score   difference

Count **forward** from Coco's score to Foxy's score...

$$\boxed{} + \boxed{} = \boxed{}$$

Coco's score   difference   Foxy's score

1 2 3 4 5 6 7 8 9 10

Fact family

A fact family is a set of three numbers that can be subtracted or added together. Fill in the blank spaces to show the two subtracting and two adding calculations for this fact family.

Let's do these together.

5

2 ⟷ 3

+

.... − ..2.. = ...

.... − ..3.. = ...

.... + ..3.. = ...

.... + ..2.. = ...

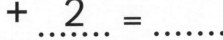

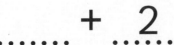

Fact family

Fill in the blank spaces to show the two
subtracting and two adding calculations
for this fact family.

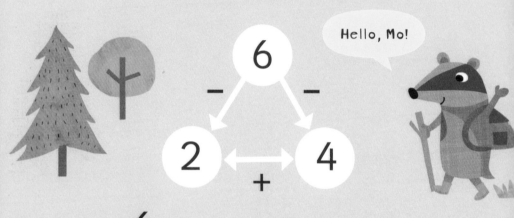

6

− −

2 ⟷ 4

+

Hello, Mo!

.6... − .... = ...

.6... − .... = ...

.2... + ... = ...

.4... + ... = ...

Fact family

A fact family is a set of three numbers that can be subtracted or added together. Fill in the blank spaces to show the two subtracting and two adding calculations for this fact family.

7

−   −

3   4

+

.... − ..3.. = ...

.... − .... = ..3..

.... + ... = ..7..

..4.. + ... = ...

Fact family

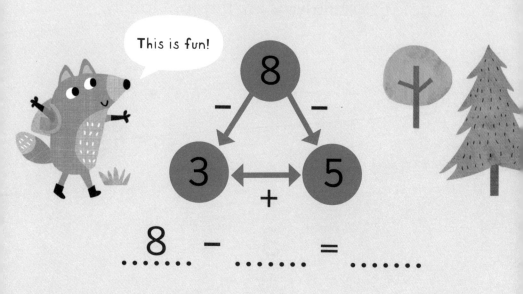

72

Fill in the blank spaces to show the two
subtracting and two adding calculations
for this fact family.

This is fun!

8

-       -

3 ⟷ 5

+

8 - .... = ...

.... - 5 = ...

.... + ... = 8

.... + 3 = ...

Fact family

A fact family is a set of three numbers that can be subtracted or added together. Fill in the blank spaces to show the two subtracting and two adding calculations for this fact family.

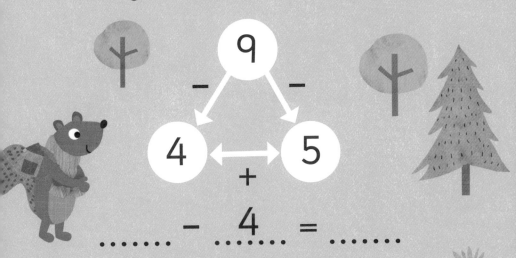

$$\ldots \ldots - \underline{4} = \ldots \ldots$$

$$\ldots \ldots - \ldots \ldots = \underline{4}$$

$$\ldots \ldots + \ldots \ldots = \underline{9}$$

$$\underline{5} + \ldots \ldots = \ldots \ldots$$

Picture subtracting

The café's selling cookies today. Look at how many cookies are left on each plate, then write the missing number to show how many the mice have bought.

5 cookies for sale

5 − ⬜ = 3

8 cookies for sale

8 − ⬜ = 4

3 cookies for sale

3 − ⬜ = 2

Picture subtracting

Look at how many sandwiches are left on each plate, then write the missing number to show how many the mice have bought.

4 sandwiches for sale

$$4 - \boxed{} = 1$$

9 sandwiches for sale

$$9 - \boxed{} = 7$$

8 sandwiches for sale

$$8 - \boxed{} = 0$$

Picture subtracting

The café's selling cupcakes today. Look at how many cupcakes are left on each plate, then write the missing number to show how many the mice have bought.

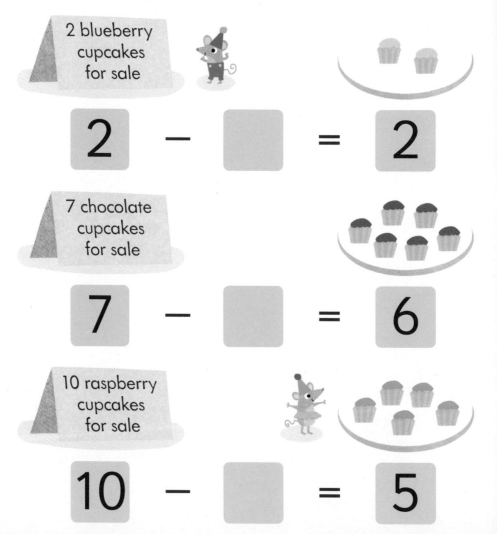

2 blueberry cupcakes for sale

2 − ☐ = 2

7 chocolate cupcakes for sale

7 − ☐ = 6

10 raspberry cupcakes for sale

10 − ☐ = 5

Picture subtracting

Look at how many tarts are left on each plate,
then write the missing number to show
how many the mice have bought.

10 tarts
for sale

$$10 - \boxed{} = 8$$

7 tarts
for sale

$$7 - \boxed{} = 2$$

6 tarts
for sale

$$6 - \boxed{} = 3$$

Missing numbers

Help Bun and her friend to fill in the missing
number in each calculation so that it is correct.

$3 - \boxed{} = 1$

$6 - \boxed{} = 5$

$8 - \boxed{} = 4$

$7 - \boxed{} = 2$

$9 - \boxed{} = 3$

$2 - \boxed{} = 0$

Now help Bun and her friend to fill in the missing numbers in these calculations, too.

$$8 - \boxed{} = 5$$

$$6 - \boxed{} = 4$$

$$10 - \boxed{} = 9$$

$$5 - \boxed{} = 1$$

$$4 - \boxed{} = 2$$

$$6 - \boxed{} = 6$$

Right or wrong?

Put a ✓ or X in the boxes by Hug and Spike's calculation to mark them right or wrong. Then turn the page.

5 – 1 = 4 ☐   3 – 2 = 1 ☐

8 – 3 = 5 ☐   7 – 4 = 2 ☐

4 – 0 = 0 ☐   10 – 3 = 8 ☐

6 – 3 = 3 ☐   5 – 5 = 0 ☐

7 – 2 = 4 ☐

9 – 5 = 6 ☐

Correcting calculations 81

Complete the other side of this page. Then help Moley to copy the calculations that are wrong into the blank boxes below, writing the correct answers instead.

☐ − ☐ = ☐

☐ − ☐ = ☐

☐ − ☐ = ☐

☐ − ☐ = ☐

☐ − ☐ = ☐

Lots of calculations

Help Squilly and Spike to fill in the missing numbers in these calculations so that they are all correct.

$4 - 2 = \boxed{}$ $9 - 9 = \boxed{}$

$8 - \boxed{} = 3$ $4 - \boxed{} = 4$

$7 - 4 = \boxed{}$ $10 - 5 = \boxed{}$

$6 - \boxed{} = 1$ $9 - \boxed{} = 3$

$10 - 3 = \boxed{}$ $7 - 2 = \boxed{}$

$6 - \boxed{} = 0$

Lots of calculations

Now help Coco and Stripe to fill in the
missing numbers in these calculations.

6 − 4 = ▢   7 − 6 = ▢

2 − ▢ = 0   8 − ▢ = 5

8 − 4 = ▢   10 − 10 = ▢

7 − ▢ = 5   3 − ▢ = 2

5 − 3 = ▢   9 − 2 = ▢

9 − ▢ = 9

Subtracting from 10

Count the vegetables in each group, then cross out the right number of them and complete the calculations to show how many are left.

 Cross out 1 carrot

 $10 - 1 = 9$

 Cross out 2 turnips

 Cross out 3 radishes

 Cross out 4 parsnips

 Cross out 5 onions

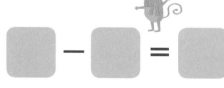

Subtracting from 10

Count the vegetables in each group, then cross out the right number of them and complete the calculations to show how many are left.

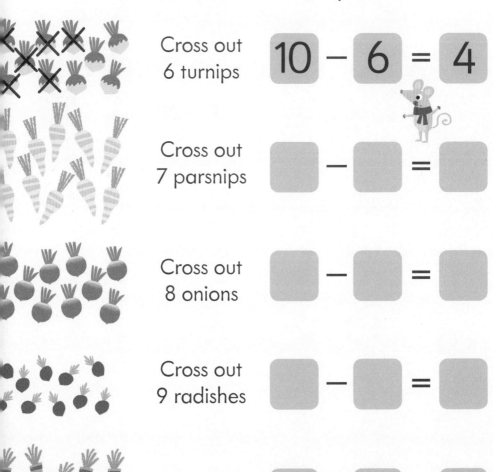

Cross out
6 turnips

$$10 - 6 = 4$$

Cross out
7 parsnips

☐ − ☐ = ☐

Cross out
8 onions

☐ − ☐ = ☐

Cross out
9 radishes

☐ − ☐ = ☐

Cross out
10 carrots

☐ − ☐ = ☐

Fact family

A fact family is a set of three numbers that can be subtracted or added together. Fill in the blank spaces to show the two subtracting and two adding calculations for this fact family.

10 – .... = ...

10 – .... = ...

1 + ... = ...

9 + ... = ...

Fact family

Fill in the blank spaces to show the two subtracting and two adding calculations for this fact family.

Can you help me with these?

10

−　　　−

2　　　8

+

...... − ..2.. = ...

...... − ..8.. = ...

...... + ..8.. = ...

...... + ..2.. = ...

Fact family

A fact family is a set of three numbers that can be subtracted or added together. Fill in the blank spaces to show the two subtracting and two adding calculations for this fact family.

10 − 7 ....

10 − .... = ...

.... − 7 = ...

.... + ... = 10

.... + 3 = ...

Fact family

89

Fill in the blank spaces to show the two subtracting and two adding calculations for this fact family.

10

− −

4 ⟷ 6

+

We can use number bonds to help!

.... − ..4.. = ...

.... − .... = ..4..

.... + ... = ..10..

..6.. + ... = ...

Fact family

A fact family is a set of three numbers that can be subtracted or added together. Fill in the blank spaces to show the two subtracting and two adding calculations for this fact family.

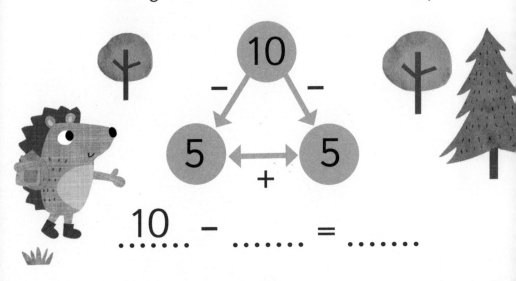

10 – .... = ...

.... – 5 = ...

.... + ... = 10

.... + 5 = ...

Number bonds for 10 91

Show Moley and Spike which numbers to add to make 10 in the first column. Then help the mice to fill in the nswers to the subtractions from 10 in the second column.

$1 + \boxed{} = 10$ $10 - 1 = \boxed{}$

$2 + \boxed{} = 10$ $10 - 2 = \boxed{}$

$3 + \boxed{} = 10$ $10 - 3 = \boxed{}$

$4 + \boxed{} = 10$ $10 - 4 = \boxed{}$

$5 + \boxed{} = 10$ $10 - 5 = \boxed{}$

Number bonds for 10

Show the mice which numbers to add to make 10 in the first column. Then help Squilly and her friend to fill in the answers to the subtractions from 10 in the second column.

6 + ☐ = 10 ¦ 10 − 6 = ☐

7 + ☐ = 10 ¦ 10 − 7 = ☐

8 + ☐ = 10 ¦ 10 − 8 = ☐

9 + ☐ = 10 ¦ 10 − 9 = ☐

10 + ☐ = 10 ¦ 10 − 10 = ☐

Subtracting quiz

Help Moley to fill in the answers to
these calculations in the boxes.

10 – 4 =

10 – 7 =

10 – 2 =

10 – 9 =

I forgot
my pen!

10 – 0 =

10 – 6 =

Subtracting quiz

Now help Coco to fill in the
answers to these calculations.

10 – 1 =

10 – 8 =

10 – 5 =

10 – 7 =

10 – 3 =

10 – 10 =

Missing numbers

Fill in the missing numbers in these subtractions from 10.

10 − ☐ = 2

10 − ☐ = 0

10 − ☐ = 4

10 − ☐ = 7

10 − ☐ = 5

Missing numbers

Now fill in the missing numbers in
these subtractions from 10, too.

10 − ☐ = 10

10 − ☐ = 6

10 − ☐ = 3

10 − ☐ = 9

10 − ☐ = 1

Number order

Starting at 20, join up the numbers in order, from highest to lowest, to finish drawing the string of Bun's kite.

Number names

Hug is matching each number to its name.
Finish drawing the lines for him.

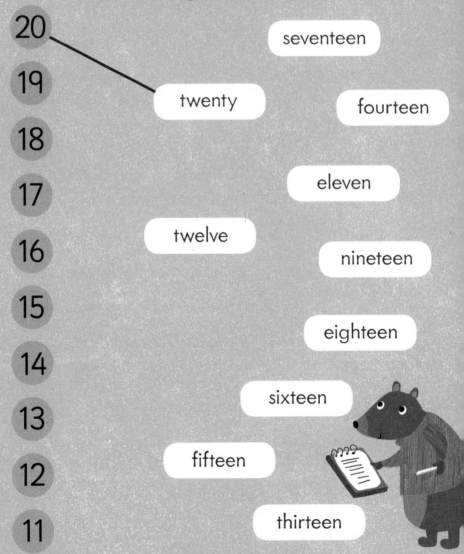

20

19

18

17

16

15

14

13

12

11

seventeen

twenty

fourteen

eleven

twelve

nineteen

eighteen

sixteen

fifteen

thirteen

Who has less?

Each animal has a different number of turnips
in their basket. Draw a circle around any
animal who has less than Hug.

11 — 12 — 13 — 14 — 15 — 16 — 17 — 18 — 19 — 20

Who has less?

Each animal has a different number of carrots
in their basket. Draw a circle around any
animal who has less than Foxy.

Foxy

14

12

16

10

7

1 – 2 – 3 – 4 – 5 – 6 – 7 – 8 – 9 –10–11–12–13–14–15–16–17–18–19–2

How many less?

The foxes want to buy less than the raccoons.
Fill in how many things the raccoons are buying,
then write how many the foxes will buy.

How many less?

102

The hedgehogs want to buy less than the rabbits.
Fill in how many things the rabbits are buying,
then write how many the hedgehogs will buy.

Rabbits

Hedgehog

I want 6 less
than you.

I'll buy 17 less
than you.

I need 11 less
than you.

How many less?

The squirrels want to buy less than the moles.
Fill in how many things the moles are buying,
then write how many the squirrels will buy.

How many less?

The badgers want to buy less than the foxes.
Fill in how many things the foxes are buying,
then write how many the badgers will buy.

Foxes

Badger

Number lines

For each number line, read how many Spike needs to subtract from the number in red, then count back and circle the number you reach.

Subtract 6 from the number in red.

11 — 12 — 13 — 14 — 15 — 16 — 17 — (18) — 19 — 20

Subtract 9 this time.

11 — 12 — 13 — 14 — 15 — 16 — 17 — 18 — 19 — (20)

Subtract 2 this time.

11 — 12 — 13 — 14 — 15 — (16) — 17 — 18 — 19 — 20

Subtract 4 this time.

11 — 12 — 13 — 14 — 15 — 16 — 17 — 18 — (19) — 20

Come on, Mo!

Number lines

For each number line, help Moley to count
back from the number in red, and
circle the number you reach.

Subtract 7 from the number in red.

11 — 12 — 13 — 14 — 15 — 16 — 17 — 18 — **19** — 20

Subtract 0 this time.

11 — **12** — 13 — 14 — 15 — 16 — 17 — 18 — 19 — 20

Subtract 5 this time.

11 — 12 — 13 — 14 — 15 — **16** — 17 — 18 — 19 — 20

Subtract 1 this time.

11 — 12 — 13 — 14 — 15 — 16 — 17 — **18** — 19 — 20

Number lines

For each number line, read how many Stripe needs to subtract from the number in red, then count back and circle the number you reach.

Subtract 3 from the number in red.

11 — 12 — 13 — 14 — 15 — 16 — **17** — 18 — 19 — 20

Subtract 6 this time.

11 — 12 — 13 — 14 — 15 — 16 — 17 — 18 — 19 — **20**

Subtract 8 this time.

11 — 12 — 13 — 14 — 15 — 16 — 17 — 18 — **19** — 20

Subtract 5 this time.

11 — 12 — 13 — 14 — 15 — 16 — 17 — **18** — 19 — 20

Number lines

For each number line, help Foxy to count
back from the number in red, and
circle the number you reach.

Subtract 4 from the number in red.

11 — 12 — 13 — 14 — 15 — **16** — 17 — 18 — 19 — 20

Subtract 1 this time.

11 — 12 — 13 — ⑭ — 15 — 16 — 17 — 18 — 19 — 20

Subtract 7 this time.

11 — 12 — 13 — 14 — 15 — 16 — 17 — **18** — 19 — 20

Subtract 2 this time.

11 — 12 — 13 — 14 — 15 — 16 — 17 — 18 — 19 — ⑳

Go, Foxy!

Subtracting quiz

Help Moley to fill in the answers
to these calculations.

19 – 1 =

16 – 5 =

18 – 4 =

15 – 3 =

17 – 2 =

20 – 8 =

Subtracting quiz

Now help Coco to fill in the
answers to these calculations.

14 – 2 =

11 – 0 =

17 – 4 =

20 – 3 =

13 – 1 =

19 – 6 =

I can do that one!

Missing numbers

Help Bun and her friend to fill in the missing
number in each calculation so that it is correct.

$$12 - \boxed{} = 11$$

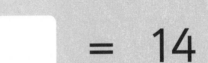

$$14 - \boxed{} = 14$$

$$19 - \boxed{} = 17$$

$$17 - \boxed{} = 13$$

$$20 - \boxed{} = 15$$

$$18 - \boxed{} = 12$$

Missing numbers

Now help Bun and her friend to fill in the missing numbers in these calculations, too.

19 − ☐ = 13

16 − ☐ = 14

20 − ☐ = 19

17 − ☐ = 12

11 − ☐ = 11

18 − ☐ = 15

Number lines

For each number line, count back from the number in red to help you complete the calculation. Then circle whether the answer is 'odd' or 'even'.

$17 - 5 =$ ....   odd / even

11 — 12 — 13 — 14 — 15 — 16 — **17** — 18 — 19 — 20

$14 - 3 =$ ....   odd / even

11 — 12 — 13 — **14** — 15 — 16 — 17 — 18 — 19 — 20

$20 - 4 =$ ....   odd / even

11 — 12 — 13 — 14 — 15 — 16 — 17 — 18 — 19 — **20**

$15 - 2 =$ ....   odd / even

11 — 12 — 13 — 14 — **15** — 16 — 17 — 18 — 19 — 20

Number lines

For each number line, count back from the number in red to help you complete the calculation. Then circle whether the answer is 'odd' or 'even'.

$17 - 3 =$ ....   odd / even

11 — 12 — 13 — 14 — 15 — 16 — 17 — 18 — 19 — 20

$19 - 2 =$ ....   odd / even

11 — 12 — 13 — 14 — 15 — 16 — 17 — 18 — 19 — 20

$20 - 5 =$ ....   odd / even

11 — 12 — 13 — 14 — 15 — 16 — 17 — 18 — 19 — 20

$18 - 0 =$ ....   odd / even

11 — 12 — 13 — 14 — 15 — 16 — 17 — 18 — 19 — 20

Difference game

The numbers that each pair of animals is holding must have a difference of 6. For each pair, write the lower number that's missing.

Difference game

The numbers that each pair of animals is holding must have a difference of 9. For each pair, write the lower number that's missing.

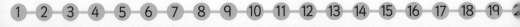

Right or wrong?

Put a ✔ or **X** in the boxes by Hug and Spike's calculations to mark them right or wrong. Then turn the page.

$19 - 5 = 16$ ☐ $16 - 4 = 12$ ☐

$13 - 3 = 10$ ☐ $20 - 9 = 13$ ☐

$17 - 0 = 0$ ☐ $12 - 2 = 10$ ☐

$20 - 6 = 14$ ☐ $17 - 4 = 14$ ☐

$15 - 3 = 12$ ☐

$18 - 8 = 11$ ☐

Correcting calculations

Complete the other side of this page. Then help Moley
to copy the calculations that are wrong into the blank
boxes below, writing the correct answers instead.

Lots of calculations

Help Foxy and Coco to fill in the missing numbers
in these calculations so that they are all correct.

$15 - 3 = \boxed{}$

$17 - 7 = \boxed{}$

$18 - \boxed{} = 8$

$14 - \boxed{} = 12$

$16 - 5 = \boxed{}$

$15 - 0 = \boxed{}$

$12 - \boxed{} = 0$

$17 - \boxed{} = 14$

$19 - 6 = \boxed{}$

$11 - 1 = \boxed{}$

$16 - \boxed{} = 0$

Lots of calculations

120

Now help Squilly and Coco to fill in the
missing numbers in these calculations.

14 − 4 = ☐

19 − 2 = ☐

19 − ☐ = 12

15 − ☐ = 0

11 − 11 = ☐

13 − 3 = ☐

16 − ☐ = 13

20 − ☐ = 12

20 − 6 = ☐

18 − 1 = ☐

17 − ☐ = 12

10 less

Count the items on each of Stripe's plates, then draw 10 less of them on Mo's plates. Use the number line to help you. Write the numbers in the boxes, then turn the page.

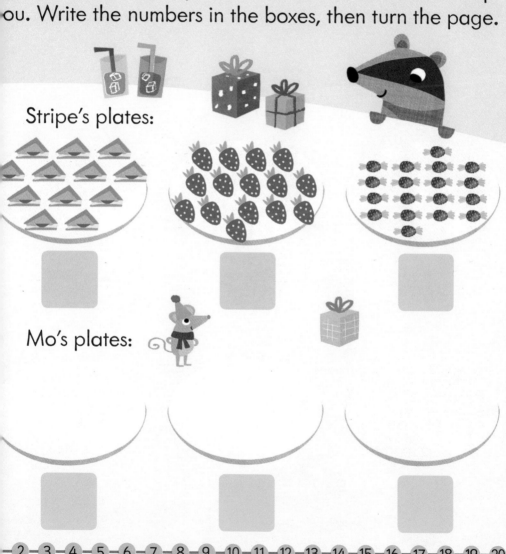

Stripe's plates:

Mo's plates:

2 — 3 — 4 — 5 — 6 — 7 — 8 — 9 — 10 — 11 — 12 — 13 — 14 — 15 — 16 — 17 — 18 — 19 — 20

10 less

Complete the other side of this page, then fill in those numbers in the calculations below.

[ ] − **10** = [ ]

Stripe's sandwiches   Mo's sandwiches

[ ] − **10** = [ ]

Stripe's strawberries   Mo's strawberries

[ ] − **10** = [ ]

Stripe's caramels   Mo's caramels

10 less

ount the items on each of Hug's plates, then draw 10 less
f them on Mo's plates. Use the number line to help you.
Write the numbers in the boxes, then turn the page.

Hug's plates:

Mo's plates:

2—3—4—5—6—7—8—9—10—11—12—13—14—15—16—17—18—19—20

Complete the other side of this page, then fill in those numbers in the calculations below.

☐ − **10** = ☐

Hug's
sausages

Mo's
sausages

☐ − **10** = ☐

Hug's
plums

Mo's
plums

☐ − **10** = ☐

Hug's
cupcakes

Mo's
cupcakes

Subtracting quiz

Help Moley to fill in the answers to
these calculations in the boxes.

$13 - 10 =$ ☐

$16 - 10 =$ ☐

$18 - 10 =$ ☐

There's
a trick to
these...

$15 - 10 =$ ☐

$17 - 10 =$ ☐

$20 - 10 =$ ☐

Subtracting quiz

Now help Coco to fill in the
answers to these calculations.

19 – 10 =

12 – 10 =

14 – 10 =

10 – 10 =

13 – 10 =

11 – 10 =

Number bonds for 20

Show the mice which numbers to add to make 20 in the first column. Then help Squilly and her friend to fill in the answers to the subtractions from 20 in the second column.

$1 +$ ☐ $= 20$ ┊ $20 - 1 =$ ☐

$2 +$ ☐ $= 20$ ┊ $20 - 2 =$ ☐

$3 +$ ☐ $= 20$ ┊ $20 - 3 =$ ☐

$4 +$ ☐ $= 20$ ┊ $20 - 4 =$ ☐

$5 +$ ☐ $= 20$ ┊ $20 - 5 =$ ☐

Number bonds for 20

Show Moley and Spike which numbers to add to make 20 in the first column. Then help the mice to fill in the answers to the subtractions from 20 in the second column

$6 +$ ☐ $= 20$ $20 - 6 =$ ☐

$7 +$ ☐ $= 20$ $20 - 7 =$ ☐

$8 +$ ☐ $= 20$ $20 - 8 =$ ☐

$9 +$ ☐ $= 20$ $20 - 9 =$ ☐

$10 +$ ☐ $= 20$ $20 - 10 =$ ☐

Number bonds for 20

Show the mice which numbers to add to make 20 in the first column. Then help Squilly and her friend to fill in the answers to the subtractions from 20 in the second column.

11 + ☐ = 20   20 − 11 = ☐

12 + ☐ = 20   20 − 12 = ☐

13 + ☐ = 20   20 − 13 = ☐

14 + ☐ = 20   20 − 14 = ☐

15 + ☐ = 20   20 − 15 = ☐

Number bonds for 20

Show Moley and Spike which numbers to add to make 20 in the first column. Then help the mice to fill in the answers to the subtractions from 20 in the second column

16 + ☐ = 20 ┊ 20 – 16 = ☐

17 + ☐ = 20 ┊ 20 – 17 = ☐

18 + ☐ = 20 ┊ 20 – 18 = ☐

19 + ☐ = 20 ┊ 20 – 19 = ☐

20 + ☐ = 20 ┊ 20 – 20 = ☐

Fact families for 20

Help Stripe to fill in numbers in the empty circles to show some fact families for 20. The two numbers you write in each set of empty circles should add up to 20.

Help Stripe to fill in numbers in the empty circles to show some fact families for 20. The two numbers you write in each set of empty circles should add up to 20.

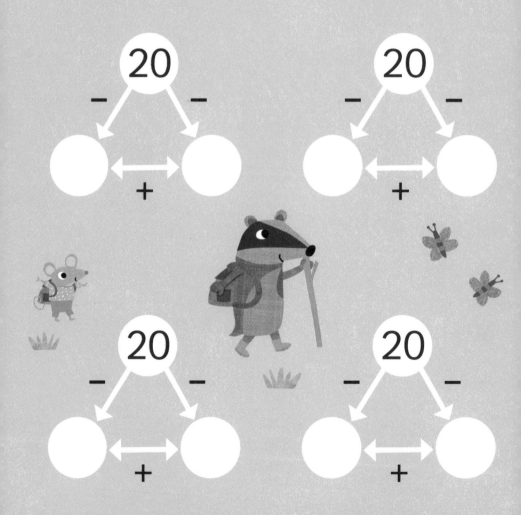

Lots of calculations

Help Squilly and Foxy to fill in the missing numbers in these calculations so that they are all correct.

17 – 5 = ☐   20 – 7 = ☐

10 – ☐ = 4   14 – ☐ = 3

13 – 5 = ☐   16 – 6 = ☐

6 – ☐ = 3   19 – ☐ = 8

11 – 6 = ☐   3 – 0 = ☐

                    8 – ☐ = 6

Lots of calculations

Now help Coco and Foxy to fill in the
missing numbers in these calculations.

12 − 5 = ☐   13 − 10 = ☐

18 − ☐ = 10   5 − ☐ = 3

16 − 15 = ☐   7 − 0 = ☐

9 − ☐ = 5   8 − ☐ = 4

20 − 20 = ☐   14 − 6 = ☐

17 − ☐ = 6

Lots of calculations

Help Bun and Spike to fill in the missing numbers in these calculations so that they are all correct.

$1 - 1 = \boxed{}$

$16 - 2 = \boxed{}$

$20 - \boxed{} = 11$

$19 - \boxed{} = 12$

$8 - 5 = \boxed{}$

$17 - 7 = \boxed{}$

$14 - \boxed{} = 10$

$9 - \boxed{} = 6$

$17 - 8 = \boxed{}$

$4 - 0 = \boxed{}$

$10 - \boxed{} = 8$

Lots of calculations

Now help Stripe and Spike to fill in the missing numbers in these calculations.

$11 - 2 = \boxed{}$

$20 - 6 = \boxed{}$

$8 - \boxed{} = 0$

$14 - \boxed{} = 4$

$15 - 5 = \boxed{}$

$19 - 13 = \boxed{}$

$17 - \boxed{} = 5$

$6 - \boxed{} = 5$

$13 - 4 = \boxed{}$

$10 - 10 = \boxed{}$

$18 - \boxed{} = 16$

Space for calculations

Space for calculations

Answers

Number order 1

Starting at 10, join up the numbers in order, from highest to lowest, to finish drawing the string of Bun's kite.

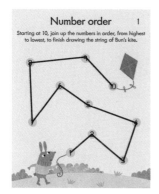

Number names 2

Hug is matching each number to its name. Finish drawing the lines for him.

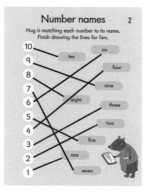

Subtract 1 3

Count the mittens in each group below, then cross out 1 of them. Write the numbers in the boxes.

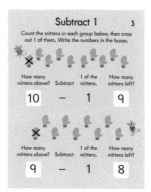

How many mittens above?	Subtract	1 of the mittens.	How many mittens left?
10	−	1	9

How many mittens above?	Subtract	1 of the mittens.	How many mittens left?
9	−	1	8

Subtract 1 4

Count the leaves in each group below, then cross out 1 of them. Write the numbers in the boxes.

How many leaves above?	Subtract	1 of the leaves.	How many leaves left?
8	−	1	7

How many leaves above?	Subtract	1 of the leaves.	How many leaves left?
7	−	1	6

Subtract 1 5

Count the bees in each group below, then cross out 1 of them. Write the numbers in the boxes.

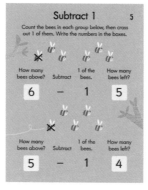

How many bees above?	Subtract	1 of the bees.	How many bees left?
6	−	1	5

How many bees above?	Subtract	1 of the bees.	How many bees left?
5	−	1	4

Subtract 1 6

Count the apples in each group below, then cross out 1 of them. Write the numbers in the boxes.

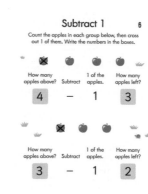

How many apples above?	Subtract	1 of the apples.	How many apples left?
4	−	1	3

How many apples above?	Subtract	1 of the apples.	How many apples left?
3	−	1	2

Subtract 1 7

Count the cakes in each group below, then cross out 1 of them. Write the numbers in the boxes.

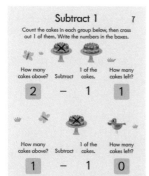

How many cakes above?	Subtract	1 of the cakes.	How many cakes left?
2	−	1	1

How many cakes above?	Subtract	1 of the cakes.	How many cakes left?
1	−	1	0

Subtract 2 8

Count the carrots in each group below, then cross out 2 of them. Write the numbers in the boxes.

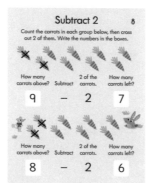

How many carrots above?	Subtract	2 of the carrots.	How many carrots left?
9	−	2	7

How many carrots above?	Subtract	2 of the carrots.	How many carrots left?
8	−	2	6

Subtract 2 9

Count the berries in each group below, then cross out 2 of them. Write the numbers in the boxes.

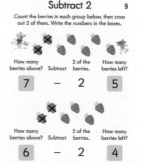

How many berries above?	Subtract	2 of the berries.	How many berries left?
7	−	2	5

How many berries above?	Subtract	2 of the berries.	How many berries left?
6	−	2	4

Answers

Subtract 2 — 10

Count the rings in each group below, then cross out 2 of them. Write the numbers in the boxes.

How many rings above?	Subtract	2 of the rings.	How many rings left?
5	−	2	3

How many rings above?	Subtract	2 of the rings.	How many rings left?
4	−	2	2

Subtract 2 — 11

Count the cups in each group below, then cross out 2 of them. Write the numbers in the boxes.

How many cups above?	Subtract	2 of the cups.	How many cups left?
3	−	2	1

How many cups above?	Subtract	2 of the cups.	How many cups left?
2	−	2	0

Number lines — 12

Help Coco to subtract 1 from each number in red. Start at the number in red on each number line, then count back one. Circle the number you reach.

1 2 3 4 5 6 7 8 9 10

1 2 3 4 5 6 7 8 9 10

1 2 3 4 5 6 7 8 9 10

1 2 3 4 5 6 7 8 9 10

Thanks for your help! −1

Number lines — 13

Help Moley to count back 2 from each number in red, and circle the number you reach.

1 2 3 4 5 6 7 8 9 10

1 2 3 4 5 6 7 8 9 10

1 2 3 4 5 6 7 8 9 10

1 2 3 4 5 6 7 8 9 10

−2

More subtracting — 14

Count the shells in each group below, then cross out how many to subtract. Write the numbers in the boxes.

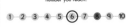

How many shells above?	Subtract	2 of the shells.	How many shells left?
5	−	2	3

How many shells above?	Subtract	6 of the shells.	How many shells left?
7	−	6	1

More subtracting — 15

Cross out how many books to subtract from each group and write the numbers in the boxes.

What big books!

How many books above?	Subtract	3 of the books.	How many books left?
6	−	3	3

How many books above?	Subtract	8 of the books.	How many books left?
8	−	8	0

More subtracting — 16

Count the socks in each group below, then cross out how many to subtract. Write the numbers in the boxes.

These aren't my socks.

How many socks above?	Subtract	5 of the socks.	How many socks left?
6	−	5	1

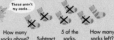

How many socks above?	Subtract	1 of the socks.	How many socks left?
8	−	1	7

More subtracting — 17

Cross out how many gifts to subtract from each group and write the numbers in the boxes.

I wonder what's inside!

How many gifts above?	Subtract	9 of the gifts.	How many gifts left?
10	−	9	1

How many gifts above?	Subtract	4 of the gifts.	How many gifts left?
9	−	4	5

More subtracting — 18

Count the fish in each group below, then cross out how many to subtract. Write the numbers in the boxes.

How many fish above?	Subtract	10 of the fish.	How many fish left?
10	−	10	0

How many fish above?	Subtract	7 of the fish.	How many fish left?
9	−	7	2

Answers

Number lines   19

Help Bun to subtract 3 from each number in red. Start at the number in red on each number line, then count back three. Circle the number you reach.

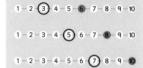

1 – 2 – ③ – 4 – 5 – ⑥ – 7 – 8 – 9 – 10

1 – 2 – 3 – 4 – ⑤ – 6 – 7 – ⑧ – 9 – 10

1 – 2 – 3 – 4 – 5 – 6 – ⑦ – 8 – 9 – ⑩

1 – ② – 3 – 4 – ⑤ – 6 – 7 – 8 – 9 – 10

–3

You're good at this!

Number lines   20

Help Foxy to count back 4 from each number in red, and circle the number you reach.

1 – 2 – 3 – 4 – ⑤ – 6 – 7 – 8 – ⑨ – 10

1 – 2 – ③ – 4 – 5 – 6 – ⑦ – 8 – 9 – 10

① – 2 – 3 – 4 – ⑤ – 6 – 7 – 8 – 9 – 10

1 – 2 – 3 – 4 – 5 – ⑥ – 7 – 8 – 9 – ⑩

–4

Who has less?   21

Each animal has a different number of apples in their basket. Draw a circle around any animal who has less than Squilly.

Squilly

6

10

4

5

7

1 – 2 – 3 – 4 – 5 – 6 – 7 – 8 – 9 – 10

Odd or even?   22

Write the answer to each calculation in the empty box and circle 'odd' or 'even' below each number. Use the number line at the bottom to help you.

5 – 1 = 4

odd /(even)   odd /(even)   odd /(even)

2 – 1 = 1

odd /(even)   odd /(even)   (odd)/ even

7 – 1 = 6

(odd)/ even   (odd)/ even   odd /(even)

1 – 2 – 3 – 4 – 5 – 6 – 7 – 8 – 9 – 10
odd even odd even odd even odd even odd even

Odd or even?   23

Write the answer to each calculation in the empty box and circle 'odd' or 'even' below each number. Use the number line at the bottom to help you.

6 – 2 = 4

odd /(even)   odd /(even)   odd /(even)

9 – 2 = 7

(odd)/ even   odd /(even)   (odd)/ even

3 – 2 = 1

(odd)/ even   odd /(even)   (odd)/ even

1 – 2 – 3 – 4 – 5 – 6 – 7 – 8 – 9 – 10
odd even odd even odd even odd even odd even

Write 1 less   24

What is 1 less than each of these numbers? Write the answers in the boxes next to them.

2	1		10	9
7	6		5	4
9	8		8	7
3	2		1	0
6	5		4	3

Write 2 less   25

What is 2 less than each of these numbers? Write the answers in the boxes next to them.

8	6		4	2
3	1		7	5
6	4		9	7
2	0		5	3

Number lines   26

For each number line, read how many Stripe needs to subtract from the number in red, then count back and circle the number you reach.

Subtract 7 from the number in red.
1 – ② – 3 – 4 – 5 – 6 – 7 – 8 – ⑨ – 10

Subtract 3 this time.
1 – 2 – ③ – 4 – 5 – ⑥ – 7 – 8 – 9 – 10

Subtract 5 this time.
1 – 2 – 3 – 4 – ⑤ – 6 – 7 – 8 – 9 – ⑩

Subtract 1 this time.
① – 2 – ③ – 4 – 5 – 6 – 7 – 8 – 9 – 10

Hello there, little bird!

Number lines   27

For each number line, help Squilly to count back from the number in red, and circle the number you reach.

Subtract 4 from the number in red.
① – 2 – 3 – 4 – ⑤ – 6 – 7 – 8 – 9 – 10

Subtract 7 this time.
1 – 2 – ③ – 4 – 5 – 6 – 7 – 8 – 9 – ⑩

Subtract 2 this time.
1 – ② – 3 – ④ – 5 – 6 – 7 – 8 – 9 – 10

Subtract 3 this time.
1 – 2 – 3 – ④ – 5 – 6 – ⑦ – 8 – 9 – 10

Answers

Number lines 28

For each number line, read how many Bun needs to subtract from the number in red, then count back and circle the number you reach.

Subtract 2 from the number in red.

Subtract 4 this time.

Subtract 1 this time.

Subtract 5 this time.

Number lines 29

For each number line, help Foxy and his friend to count back from the number in red, and circle the number you reach.

Subtract 5 from the number in red.
$1 - 2 - 3 - \textcircled{4} - 5 - 6 - 7 - 8 - \textcircled{9} - 10$

Subtract 2 this time.
$\textcircled{1} - 2 - \textcircled{3} - 4 - 5 - 6 - 7 - 8 - 9 - 10$

Subtract 4 this time.
$1 - 2 - \textcircled{3} - 4 - 5 - 6 - \textcircled{7} - 8 - 9 - 10$

Subtract 6 this time.
$1 - \textcircled{2} - 3 - 4 - 5 - 6 - 7 - \textcircled{8} - 9 - 10$

The right order 30

Mark these calculations to see if the numbers in them are in the right order. Put a ✓ or a **X** in each box. Try crossing out the fruit to help you.

$5 - 3 = 2$ ✓ $3 - 5 = 2$ **X**

$7 - 4 = 3$ ✓ $4 - 7 = 3$ **X**

$8 - 2 = 6$ ✓ $2 - 8 = 6$ **X**

The right order 31

Mark these calculations to see if the numbers in them are in the right order. Put a ✓ or a **X** in each box. Try crossing out the fruit to help you.

$9 - 7 = 2$ ✓ $7 - 9 = 2$ **X**

$2 - 6 = 4$ **X** $6 - 2 = 4$ ✓

$3 - 4 = 1$ **X** $4 - 3 = 1$ ✓

The right order 32

Mark these calculations to see if the numbers in them are in the right order. Put a ✓ or a **X** in each box. Try crossing out the fruit to help you.

$10 - 7 = 3$ ✓ $7 - 10 = 3$ **X**

$9 - 4 = 5$ ✓ $4 - 9 = 5$ **X**

$4 - 2 = 2$ ✓ $2 - 4 = 2$ **X**

The right order 33

Mark these calculations to see if the numbers in them are in the right order. Put a ✓ or a **X** in each box. Try crossing out the fruit to help you.

$3 - 9 = 6$ **X** $9 - 3 = 6$ ✓

$5 - 2 = 3$ ✓ $2 - 5 = 3$ **X**

$10 - 1 = 9$ ✓ $1 - 10 = 9$ **X**

Balance beams 34

To balance, these beams should have the same number of oranges on each side. Count the oranges – if one side has more, cross out oranges from that side.

Example:

Balance beams 35

Count the cupcakes on each beam. If one side has more, cross out cupcakes from that side.

Example:
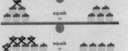

Balance beams 36

To balance, these beams should have the same number of acorns on each side. Count the acorns – if one side has more, cross out acorns from that side.

Example:
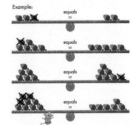

Answers

Balance beams 37

Count the teacups on each beam.
If one side has more, cross out
teacups from that side.

Example:

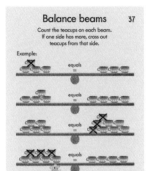

Balance beams 38

For each beam, cross out the number of marbles shown in
red below it. Then draw marbles on the other side of the
beam until it balances, and complete the calculation.

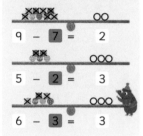

$9 - 7 = 2$

$5 - 2 = 3$

$6 - 3 = 3$

Balance beams 39

For each beam, cross out the number of mushrooms shown
in red below it. Then draw mushrooms on the other side of
the beam until it balances, and complete the calculation.

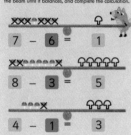

$7 - 6 = 1$

$8 - 3 = 5$

$4 - 1 = 3$

Balance beams 40

For each beam, cross out the number of gifts shown in
red below it. Then draw gifts on the other side of the
beam until it balances, and complete the calculation.

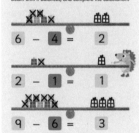

$6 - 4 = 2$

$2 - 1 = 1$

$9 - 6 = 3$

Balance beams 41

For each beam, cross out the number of watermelon slices
shown in red below it. Then draw slices on the other side of
the beam until it balances, and complete the calculation.

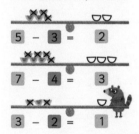

$5 - 3 = 2$

$7 - 4 = 3$

$3 - 2 = 1$

Number lines 42

Help Moley to count back from the number in red
on each number line to find the answers to the
calculations. Write the answers on the dotted lines.

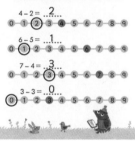

$4 - 2 = 2$

$6 - 5 = 1$

$7 - 4 = 3$

$3 - 3 = 0$

Number lines 43

Help Spike to count back from each number
in red, and write the answers to the
calculations on the dotted lines.

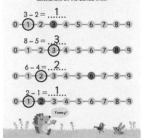

$3 - 2 = 1$

$8 - 5 = 3$

$6 - 4 = 2$

$2 - 1 = 1$

Number lines 44

Help Foxy to count back from the number in red
on each number line to find the answers to the
calculations. Write the answers on the dotted lines.

$1 - 1 = 0$

$5 - 4 = 1$

$9 - 5 = 4$

$7 - 2 = 5$

Number lines 45

Help Coco to count back from each number
in red, and write the answers to the
calculations on the dotted lines.

$4 - 4 = 0$

$8 - 6 = 2$

$7 - 3 = 4$

$5 - 2 = 3$

Answers

Picture subtracting 46

Fill in how many gifts are on each table. Cross out the number of gifts to subtract, then write how many are left.

$9 - 5 = 4$
gifts on table   gifts   gifts left

$7 - 3 = 4$
gifts on table   gifts   gifts left

$8 - 6 = 2$
gifts on table   gifts   gifts left

Picture subtracting 47

Fill in how many cupcakes are on each table. Cross out the number of cupcakes to subtract, then write how many are left.

$7 - 4 = 3$
cupcakes on table   cupcakes   cupcakes left

$8 - 1 = 7$
cupcakes on table   cupcakes   cupcakes left

$9 - 7 = 2$
cupcakes on table   cupcakes   cupcakes left

Picture subtracting 48

Count the fruit on each shelf, then cross out the number of them the mice want to buy. Fill in the numbers, and write how many are left to complete the calculations.

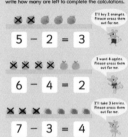

I'll buy 2 oranges. Please cross them out for me.

$5 - 2 = 3$

I want 4 apples. Please cross them out for me.

$6 - 4 = 2$

I'll take 3 berries. Please cross them out for me.

$7 - 3 = 4$

Picture subtracting 49

Count the fruit on each shelf, then cross out the number of them the mice want to buy. Fill in the numbers, and write how many are left to complete the calculations.

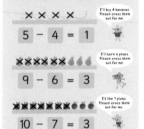

I'll buy 4 bananas. Please cross them out for me.

$5 - 4 = 1$

I'll have 6 pears. Please cross them out for me.

$9 - 6 = 3$

I'd like 7 plums. Please cross them out for me.

$10 - 7 = 3$

Picture subtracting 50

Fill in how many butterflies Mo can see. Then write how many have flown away, and how many butterflies are left.

a. I spy seven butterflies. Three of them have gone now.

$7 - 3 = 4$

b. I can see four butterflies. Now one has flown away.

$4 - 1 = 3$

c. I've spotted five butterflies. Oh, now there are two less.

$5 - 2 = 3$

Picture subtracting 51

Fill in how many bees Mo can see. Then write how many have flown away, and how many bees are left.

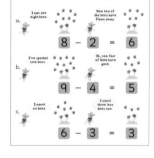

a. I can see eight bees. Now two of the bees have flown away.

$8 - 2 = 6$

b. I've spotted nine bees. Oh, now four of them have gone.

$9 - 4 = 5$

c. I count six bees. I count three less bees now.

$6 - 3 = 3$

Number lines 52

For each number line, count back from the number in red to help you complete the calculation. Then circle whether the answer is 'odd' or 'even'.

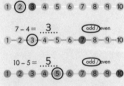

$3 - 1 = 2$ odd (even)
1 (2) 3 4 5 6 7 8 9 10

$7 - 4 = 3$ (odd) even
1 2 (3) 4 5 6 7 8 9 10

$10 - 5 = 5$ (odd) even
1 2 3 4 (5) 6 7 8 9 10

$6 - 2 = 4$ odd (even)
1 2 3 (4) 5 6 7 8 9 10

Number lines 53

For each number line, count back from the number in red to help you complete the calculation. Then circle whether the answer is 'odd' or 'even'.

$9 - 6 = 3$ (odd) even
1 2 (3) 4 5 6 7 8 9 10

$4 - 3 = 1$ (odd) even
(1) 2 3 4 5 6 7 8 9 10

$5 - 2 = 3$ (odd) even
1 2 (3) 4 5 6 7 8 9 10

$8 - 4 = 4$ odd (even)
1 2 3 (4) 5 6 7 8 9 10

Subtracting quiz 54

Help Foxy to fill in the answers to these calculations in the boxes.

$7 - 3 = 4$

$5 - 4 = 1$

$9 - 5 = 4$

$6 - 3 = 3$

$8 - 6 = 2$

$4 - 1 = 3$

Answers

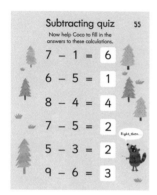

Subtracting quiz 55

Now help Coco to fill in the answers to these calculations.

7 – 1 = 6

6 – 5 = 1

8 – 4 = 4

7 – 5 = 2

5 – 3 = 2

9 – 6 = 3

Right, then.

Subtracting nothing 56

Help Stripe and Spike to fill in the answers to these calculations in the boxes.

6 – 0 = 6

3 – 0 = 3

9 – 0 = 9

7 – 0 = 7

1 – 0 = 1

Subtracting everything 57

Now help Moley to fill in the answers to these calculations.

8 – 8 = 0

4 – 4 = 0

2 – 2 = 0

7 – 7 = 0

5 – 5 = 0

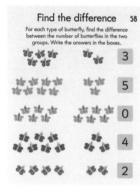

Find the difference 58

For each type of butterfly, find the difference between the number of butterflies in the two groups. Write the answers in the boxes.

3

5

0

4

2

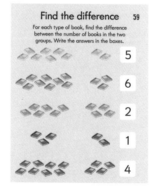

Find the difference 59

For each type of book, find the difference between the number of books in the two groups. Write the answers in the boxes.

5

6

2

1

4

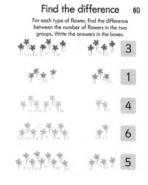

Find the difference 60

For each type of flower, find the difference between the number of flowers in the two groups. Write the answers in the boxes.

3

1

4

6

5

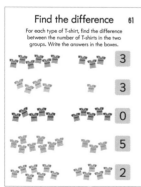

Find the difference 61

For each type of T-shirt, find the difference between the number of T-shirts in the two groups. Write the answers in the boxes.

3

3

0

5

2

Difference game 62

The numbers that each pair of animals is holding must have a difference of 3. For each pair, write the lower number that's missing.

6 3

10 7

4 1

3 0

7 4

9 6

1 – 2 – 3 – 4 – 5 – 6 – 7 – 8 – 9 – 10

Find the difference 63

Each hoop scores one point. Find the difference between each pair's scores. Use the number line at the bottom to count back from the higher score to the lower score.

4
Moley's score

2
Spike's score

2
difference

6
Coco's score

3
Foxy's score

3
difference

1 – 2 – 3 – 4 – 5 – 6 – 7 – 8 – 9 – 10

Answers

Find the difference 64

The animals are playing hoops again. Find the difference between each pair's scores, using the number line to help you.

8 Moley's score **7** Spike's score **1** difference

9 Coco's score **5** Foxy's score **4** difference

1—2—3—4—5—6—7—8—9—10

Find the difference 65

Find the difference between Squilly and Hug's scores for each pair of targets. Use the number line at the bottom to count back from the higher score to the lower score.

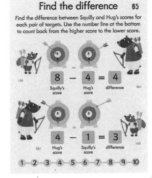

$8 - 4 = 4$
Squilly's score Hug's score difference

$4 - 1 = 3$
Hug's score Squilly's score difference

1 2 3 4 5 6 7 8 9 10

Find the difference 66

Squilly and Hug are taking another turn. Find the difference between their scores for each pair of targets, using the number line to help you.

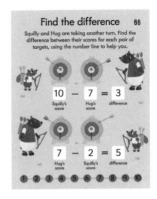

$10 - 7 = 3$
Squilly's score Hug's score difference

$7 - 2 = 5$
Hug's score Squilly's score difference

1 2 3 4 5 6 7 8 9 10

Same difference 67

Write the animals' long jump scores in the correct boxes in each calculation. Then count along the number line to find the difference, and write it in the green boxes.

Count **back** from Foxy's score to Coco's score...

$7 - 3 = 4$
Foxy's score Coco's score difference

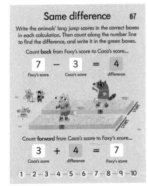

Count **forward** from Coco's score to Foxy's score...

$3 + 4 = 7$
Coco's score difference Foxy's score

1 — 2 — 3 — 4 — 5 — 6 — 7 — 8 — 9 — 10

Same difference 68

The animals are jumping again. Write their scores in the correct boxes in each calculation. Then count along the number line to write the difference in the blue boxes.

Count **back** from Foxy's score to Coco's score...

$9 - 4 = 5$
Foxy's score Coco's score difference

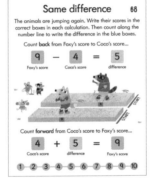

Count **forward** from Coco's score to Foxy's score...

$4 + 5 = 9$
Coco's score difference Foxy's score

1 2 3 4 5 6 7 8 9 10

Fact family 69

A fact family is a set of three numbers that can be subtracted or added together. Fill in the blank spaces to show the two subtracting and two adding calculations for this fact family.

Let's do these together

5

2 + 3

$5 - 2 = 3$

$5 - 3 = 2$

$2 + 3 = 5$

$3 + 2 = 5$

Fact family 70

Fill in the blank spaces to show the two subtracting and two adding calculations for this fact family.

Hello, Ma!

6

2 + 4

$6 - 2 = 4$

$6 - 4 = 2$

$2 + 4 = 6$

$4 + 2 = 6$

Fact family 71

A fact family is a set of three numbers that can be subtracted or added together. Fill in the blank spaces to show the two subtracting and two adding calculations for this fact family.

7

3 + 4

$7 - 3 = 4$

$7 - 4 = 3$

$3 + 4 = 7$

$4 + 3 = 7$

Fact family 72

Fill in the blank spaces to show the two subtracting and two adding calculations for this fact family.

This is fun!

8

3 + 5

$8 - 3 = 5$

$8 - 5 = 3$

$3 + 5 = 8$

$5 + 3 = 8$

Answers

Fact family 73

A fact family is a set of three numbers that can be subtracted or added together. Fill in the blank spaces to show the two subtracting and two adding calculations for this fact family.

$$9 - 4 = 5$$
$$9 - 5 = 4$$
$$4 + 5 = 9$$
$$5 + 4 = 9$$

Picture subtracting 74

The café's selling cookies today. Look at how many cookies are left on each plate, then write the missing number to show how many the mice have bought.

5 cookies for sale
$$5 - 2 = 3$$

8 cookies for sale
$$8 - 4 = 4$$

3 cookies for sale
$$3 - 1 = 2$$

Picture subtracting 75

Look at how many sandwiches are left on each plate, then write the missing number to show how many the mice have bought.

4 sandwiches for sale
$$4 - 3 = 1$$

9 sandwiches for sale
$$9 - 2 = 7$$

8 sandwiches for sale
$$8 - 8 = 0$$

Picture subtracting 76

The café's selling cupcakes today. Look at how many cupcakes are left on each plate, then write the missing number to show how many the mice have bought.

2 blueberry cupcakes for sale
$$2 - 0 = 2$$

7 chocolate cupcakes for sale
$$7 - 1 = 6$$

10 raspberry cupcakes for sale
$$10 - 5 = 5$$

Picture subtracting 77

Look at how many tarts are left on each plate, then write the missing number to show how many the mice have bought.

10 tarts for sale
$$10 - 2 = 8$$

7 tarts for sale
$$7 - 5 = 2$$

6 tarts for sale
$$6 - 3 = 3$$

Missing numbers 78

Help Bun and her friend to fill in the missing number in each calculation so that it is correct.

$$3 - 2 = 1$$
$$6 - 1 = 5$$
$$8 - 4 = 4$$
$$7 - 5 = 2$$
$$9 - 6 = 3$$
$$2 - 2 = 0$$

Missing numbers 79

Now help Bun and her friend to fill in the missing numbers in these calculations, too.

$$8 - 3 = 5$$
$$6 - 2 = 4$$
$$10 - 1 = 9$$
$$5 - 4 = 1$$
$$4 - 2 = 2$$
$$6 - 0 = 6$$

Right or wrong? 80

Put a ✓ or X in the boxes by Hug and Spike's calculations to mark them right or wrong. Then turn the page.

$$5 - 1 = 4 \quad ✓$$
$$8 - 3 = 5 \quad ✓$$
$$4 - 0 = 0 \quad X$$
$$6 - 3 = 3 \quad ✓$$
$$7 - 2 = 4 \quad X$$
$$9 - 5 = 6 \quad X$$

$$3 - 2 = 1 \quad ✓$$
$$7 - 4 = 2 \quad X$$
$$10 - 3 = 8 \quad X$$
$$5 - 5 = 0 \quad ✓$$

Correcting calculations 81

Complete the other side of this page. Then help Moley to copy the calculations that are wrong into the blank boxes below, writing the correct answers instead.

$$4 - 0 = 4$$
$$7 - 2 = 5$$
$$9 - 5 = 4$$
$$7 - 4 = 3$$
$$10 - 3 = 7$$

Answers

Lots of calculations   82

Help Squilly and Spike to fill in the missing numbers in these calculations so that they are all correct.

$4 - 2 = 2$ $9 - 9 = 0$

$8 - 5 = 3$ $4 - 0 = 4$

$7 - 4 = 3$ $10 - 5 = 5$

$6 - 5 = 1$ $9 - 6 = 3$

$10 - 3 = 7$ $7 - 2 = 5$

$6 - 6 = 0$

Lots of calculations   83

Now help Coco and Stripe to fill in the missing numbers in these calculations.

$6 - 4 = 2$ $7 - 6 = 1$

$2 - 2 = 0$ $8 - 3 = 5$

$8 - 4 = 4$ $10 - 10 = 0$

$7 - 2 = 5$ $3 - 1 = 2$

$5 - 3 = 2$ $9 - 2 = 7$

$9 - 0 = 9$

Subtracting from 10   84

Count the vegetables in each group, then cross out the right number of them and complete the calculations to show how many are left.

Cross out 1 carrot $10 - 1 = 9$

Cross out 2 turnips $10 - 2 = 8$

Cross out 3 radishes $10 - 3 = 7$

Cross out 4 parsnips $10 - 4 = 6$

Cross out 5 onions $10 - 5 = 5$

Subtracting from 10   85

Count the vegetables in each group, then cross out the right number of them and complete the calculations to show how many are left.

Cross out 6 turnips $10 - 6 = 4$

Cross out 7 parsnips $10 - 7 = 3$

Cross out 8 onions $10 - 8 = 2$

Cross out 9 radishes $10 - 9 = 1$

Cross out 10 carrots $10 - 10 = 0$

Fact family   86

A fact family is a set of three numbers that can be subtracted or added together. Fill in the blank spaces to show the two subtracting and two adding calculations for this fact family.

10
1   9

$10 - 1 = 9$

$10 - 9 = 1$

$1 + 9 = 10$

$9 + 1 = 10$

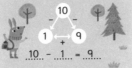

Fact family   87

Fill in the blank spaces to show the two subtracting and two adding calculations for this fact family.

Can you help me with these?

10
2   8

$10 - 2 = 8$

$10 - 8 = 2$

$2 + 8 = 10$

$8 + 2 = 10$

Fact family   88

A fact family is a set of three numbers that can be subtracted or added together. Fill in the blank spaces to show the two subtracting and two adding calculations for this fact family.

10
3   7

$10 - 3 = 7$

$10 - 7 = 3$

$3 + 7 = 10$

$7 + 3 = 10$

Fact family   89

Fill in the blank spaces to show the two subtracting and two adding calculations for this fact family.

We can use number bonds to help!

10
4   6

$10 - 4 = 6$

$10 - 6 = 4$

$4 + 6 = 10$

$6 + 4 = 10$

Fact family   90

A fact family is a set of three numbers that can be subtracted or added together. Fill in the blank spaces to show the two subtracting and two adding calculations for this fact family.

10
5   5

$10 - 5 = 5$

$10 - 5 = 5$

$5 + 5 = 10$

$5 + 5 = 10$

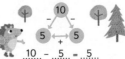

Answers

Number bonds for 10   91

Show Moley and Spike which numbers to add to make 10 in the first column. Then help the mice to fill in the answers to the subtractions from 10 in the second column.

1 + 9 = 10   10 – 1 = 9

2 + 8 = 10   10 – 2 = 8

3 + 7 = 10   10 – 3 = 7

4 + 6 = 10   10 – 4 = 6

5 + 5 = 10   10 – 5 = 5

Number bonds for 10   92

Show the mice which numbers to add to make 10 in the first column. Then help Squilly and her friend to fill in the answers to the subtractions from 10 in the second column.

6 + 4 = 10   10 – 6 = 4

7 + 3 = 10   10 – 7 = 3

8 + 2 = 10   10 – 8 = 2

9 + 1 = 10   10 – 9 = 1

10 + 0 = 10   10 – 10 = 0

Subtracting quiz   93

Help Moley to fill in the answers to these calculations in the boxes.

10 – 4 = 6

10 – 7 = 3

10 – 2 = 8

10 – 9 = 1

10 – 0 = 10

10 – 6 = 4

I forgot my pen!

Subtracting quiz   94

Now help Coco to fill in the answers to these calculations.

10 – 1 = 9

10 – 8 = 2

10 – 5 = 5

10 – 7 = 3

10 – 3 = 7

10 – 10 = 0

Missing numbers   95

Fill in the missing numbers in these subtractions from ten.

10 – 8 = 2

10 – 10 = 0

10 – 6 = 4

10 – 3 = 7

10 – 5 = 5

Missing numbers   96

Now fill in the missing numbers in these subtractions from ten, too.

10 – 0 = 10

10 – 4 = 6

10 – 7 = 3

10 – 1 = 9

10 – 9 = 1

Number order   97

Starting at 20, join up the numbers in order, from highest to lowest, to finish drawing the string of Bun's kite.

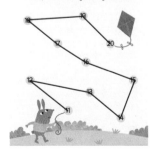

Number names   98

Hug is matching each number to its name. Finish drawing the lines for him.

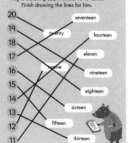

20 — twenty
19 — nineteen
18 — eighteen
17 — seventeen
16 — sixteen
15 — fifteen
14 — fourteen
13 — thirteen
12 — twelve
11 — eleven

Who has less?   99

Each animal has a different number of turnips in their basket. Draw a circle around any animal who has less than Hug.

11 – 12 – 13 – 14 – 15 – 16 – 17 – 18 – 19 – 20

Answers

Who has less? 100
Each animal has a different number of carrots in their basket. Draw a circle around any animal who has less than Foxy.

How many less? 101
The foxes want to buy less than the raccoons. Fill in how many things the raccoons are buying, then write how many the foxes will buy.

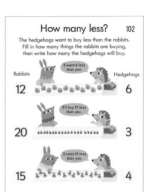

How many less? 102
The hedgehogs want to buy less than the rabbits. Fill in how many things the rabbits are buying, then write how many the hedgehogs will buy.

How many less? 103
The squirrels want to buy less than the moles. Fill in how many things the moles are buying, then write how many the squirrels will buy.

How many less? 104
The badgers want to buy less than the foxes. Fill in how many things the foxes are buying, then write how many the badgers will buy.

Number lines 105
For each number line, read how many Spike needs to subtract from the number in red, then count back and circle the number you reach.

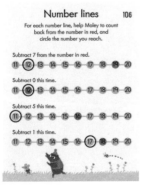

Number lines 106
For each number line, help Moley to count back from the number in red, and circle the number you reach.

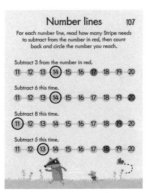

Number lines 107
For each number line, read how many Stripe needs to subtract from the number in red, then count back and circle the number you reach.

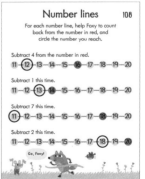

Number lines 108
For each number line, help Foxy to count back from the number in red, and circle the number you reach.

Answers

Subtracting quiz 109
Help Moley to fill in the answers to these calculations.

19 – 1 = 18
16 – 5 = 11
18 – 4 = 14
15 – 3 = 12
17 – 2 = 15
20 – 8 = 12

Subtracting quiz 110
Now help Coco to fill in the answers to these calculations.

14 – 2 = 12
11 – 0 = 11
17 – 4 = 13
20 – 3 = 17
13 – 1 = 12
19 – 6 = 13

I can do that one!

Missing numbers 111
Help Bun and her friend to fill in the missing number in each calculation so that it is correct.

12 – 1 = 11
14 – 0 = 14
19 – 2 = 17
17 – 4 = 13
20 – 5 = 15
18 – 6 = 12

Missing numbers 112
Now help Bun and her friend to fill in the missing numbers in these calculations.

19 – 6 = 13
16 – 2 = 14
20 – 1 = 19
17 – 5 = 12
11 – 0 = 11
18 – 3 = 15

Number lines 113
For each number line, count back from the number in red to help you complete the calculation. Then circle whether the answer is 'odd' or 'even'.

17 – 5 = 12   odd (even)
11 (12) 13 14 15 16 (17) 18 19 20

14 – 3 = 11   (odd) even
(11) 12 13 (14) 15 16 17 18 19 20

20 – 4 = 16   odd (even)
11 12 13 14 15 (16) 17 18 19 (20)

15 – 2 = 13   (odd) even
11 12 (13) 14 (15) 16 17 18 19 20

Number lines 114
For each number line, count back from the number in red to help you complete the calculation. Then circle whether the answer is 'odd' or 'even'.

17 – 3 = 14   odd (even)
(11) (12) (13) (14) 15 16 (17) 18 (19) 20

19 – 2 = 17   (odd) even
11 12 13 14 15 16 (17) 18 (19) 20

20 – 5 = 15   (odd) even
11 12 13 14 (15) 16 17 18 19 (20)

18 – 0 = 18   odd (even)
11 12 13 14 15 16 17 (18) 19 20

Difference game 115
The numbers that each pair of animals is holding must have a difference of 6. For each pair, write the lower number that's missing.

16 10   10 4
11 5   13 7
14 8   19 13
17 11   8 2

1 2 3 4 5 6 7 8 9 10 11 12 13 14 15 16 17 18 19 20

Difference game 116
The numbers that each pair of animals is holding must have a difference of 9. For each pair, write the lower number that's missing.

16 7   18 9
10 1   13 4
17 8   19 10
14 5   11 2

Right or wrong? 117
Put a ✓ or X in the boxes by Hug and Spike's calculations to mark them right or wrong. Then turn the page.

19 – 5 = 16 X   16 – 4 = 12 ✓
13 – 3 = 10 ✓   20 – 9 = 13 X
17 – 0 = 0   X   12 – 2 = 10 ✓
20 – 6 = 14 ✓   17 – 4 = 14 X
15 – 3 = 12 ✓
18 – 8 = 11 X

Answers

Correcting calculations 118

Complete the other side of this page. Then help Moley to copy the calculations that are wrong into the blank boxes below, writing the correct answers instead.

19 – 5 = 14

17 – 0 = 17

18 – 8 = 10

20 – 9 = 11

17 – 4 = 13

Lots of calculations 119

Help Foxy and Coco to fill in the missing numbers in these calculations so that they are all correct.

15 – 3 = 12

18 – 10 = 8

16 – 5 = 11

12 – 12 = 0

19 – 6 = 13

17 – 7 = 10

14 – 2 = 12

15 – 0 = 15

17 – 3 = 14

11 – 1 = 10

16 – 16 = 0

Lots of calculations 120

Now help Squilly and Coco to fill in the missing numbers in these calculations.

14 – 4 = 10

19 – 7 = 12

11 – 11 = 0

16 – 3 = 13

20 – 6 = 14

17 – 5 = 12

19 – 2 = 17

15 – 15 = 0

13 – 3 = 10

20 – 8 = 12

18 – 1 = 17

10 less 121

Count the items on each of Stripe's plates, then draw 10 less of them on Mo's plates. Use the number line to help you. Write the numbers in the boxes, then turn the page.

Stripe's plates:

12   15   18

Mo's plates:

2   5   8

1-2-3-4-5-6-7-8-9-10-11-12-13-14-15-16-17-18-19-20

10 less 122

Complete the other side of this page, then fill in those numbers in the calculations below.

12 – 10 = 2

Stripe's sandwiches   Mo's sandwiches

15 – 10 = 5

Stripe's strawberries   Mo's strawberries

18 – 10 = 8

Stripe's caramels   Mo's caramels

10 less 123

Count the items on each of Hug's plates, then draw 10 less of them on Mo's plates. Use the number line to help you. Write the numbers in the boxes, then turn the page.

Hug's plates:

14   13   11

Mo's plates:

4   3   1

1-2-3-4-5-6-7-8-9-10-11-12-13-14-15-16-17-18-19-20

10 less 124

Complete the other side of this page, then fill in those numbers in the calculations below.

14 – 10 = 4

Hug's sausages   Mo's sausages

13 – 10 = 3

Hug's plums   Mo's plums

11 – 10 = 1

Hug's cupcakes   Mo's cupcakes

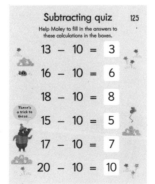

Subtracting quiz 125

Help Moley to fill in the answers to these calculations in the boxes.

13 – 10 = 3

16 – 10 = 6

18 – 10 = 8

There's a trick to these.

15 – 10 = 5

17 – 10 = 7

20 – 10 = 10

Subtracting quiz 126

Now help Coco to fill in the answers to these calculations.

19 – 10 = 9

12 – 10 = 2

14 – 10 = 4

10 – 10 = 0

13 – 10 = 3

11 – 10 = 1

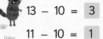